MW01535027

TWENTY-THREE

TWENTY-THREE

RICHARD KELLEY

iUniverse LLC
Bloomington

TWENTY-THREE

Copyright © 2014 Richard Kelley.

All rights reserved. No part of this book may be used or reproduced by any means, graphic, electronic, or mechanical, including photocopying, recording, taping or by any information storage retrieval system without the written permission of the publisher except in the case of brief quotations embodied in critical articles and reviews.

This is a work of fiction. All of the characters, names, incidents, organizations, and dialogue in this novel are either the products of the author's imagination or are used fictitiously.

iUniverse books may be ordered through booksellers or by contacting:

iUniverse LLC
1663 Liberty Drive
Bloomington, IN 47403
www.iuniverse.com
1-800-Authors (1-800-288-4677)

Because of the dynamic nature of the Internet, any web addresses or links contained in this book may have changed since publication and may no longer be valid. The views expressed in this work are solely those of the author and do not necessarily reflect the views of the publisher, and the publisher hereby disclaims any responsibility for them.

Any people depicted in stock imagery provided by Thinkstock are models, and such images are being used for illustrative purposes only. Certain stock imagery © Thinkstock.

Cover photograph by Richard Kelley

ISBN: 978-1-4917-2582-5 (sc)
ISBN: 978-1-4917-2586-3 (e)

Printed in the United States of America.

iUniverse rev. date: 02/20/2014

ONE

BASKETBALLS

Somewhere along the plane ride I'd fallen asleep. The flight attendant woke me up to tell me that I've arrived at my destination.

I straighten up in my seat and I thank the flight attendant who smiles gently at me, I smile back and then I quickly shake off this final act of tenderness. There isn't going to be anymore of that. I need to get focused on what's ahead of me. If I'm going to make it through this I can't allow myself to be soft.

Alright, I'm ready.

All the other passengers on the plane start to gather up their equipment, picking up their rifles and bayonets, slinging their duffle bags across their backs and tossing their rucksacks across their chests.

Every one of us is moving in silence as we get ready to walk off the plane.

Then the flight attendants tell us to sit back down. We need to wait while they determine if we are going need any chemical equipment before getting off the plane. We stay standing, waiting while they discover if there has been a recent chemical alarm. After the silent minutes tick by, they tell us it's all clear and we aren't going to need our chemical suits or protective masks.

This is my last glimpse of civilization, my last taste of freedom for the next 180 days. I take it all in, trying to memorize every moment of it.

I look each and every flight attendant in the eyes as I pass by them, trying to see if I can read their thoughts. Our lives are so different, the lives of myself and these flight attendants.

We head to the door one by one, with the overly friendly flight attendants wishing a farewell to each and every one of us as we trail off the plane, as if this had been a real flight to a real location.

They're dropping us off in a war and then they're heading back home to their safe, luxurious, free lives.

I can't help wondering what thoughts are running through their heads at this very moment. Are they soaking up this moment the same way I am, or are they just thinking about getting the hell out of here as quickly as they came. Damn. I envy these flight attendants. Did I make the right decision? What have I gotten myself into? Maybe joining the military to pay for college wasn't such a good idea after all.

Is it too late to change my mind?

There's a single file line of soldiers behind me pushing me forward. This is it. I stand still for one more brief moment. My final moment of before and after. I know my next step is going to be a step into a new life. My old life is gone and my life will never be the same again. I know my life is about to change forever.

As I walk off the plane, I turn around and take one last look at the plane. I see the flight attendant close the door behind me. I turn back around and I keep walking. There's no more looking back now.

I had expected the heat to hit me first, but to my surprise, it was the sun. It's so bright. I feel like I'm walking on the sun. I'm blinded by the brightness, I have to squint my eyes almost to the point where they're closed. Then the heat hits me, it's overwhelming, it doesn't just take my breath away, it gags me. The heat tries it's best to strangle me, but it doesn't win.

We all walk in a line from the plane to the airplane hanger. This will be my new residence for the time being. Great. I'm going to live in an airplane hanger.

We walk down the runway and in the distance I see a basketball court with several soldiers playing basketball. They look like they're just passing the time, playing a game. It's just an ordinary day for them.

As we get closer I notice all the players are wearing chemical masks. We walk across the court and right through their game. They don't even acknowledge us, the soldiers just keep playing while we parade through their game. Everything feels like it's happening in slow motion. The walk though their game feels like a lifetime. I feel lost, misplaced. I have no idea what's in store for me. I'm so focused on this moment in time, I'm not able to think clearly.

Everyone in our line walks by without a word, we exchange glances with one another, wondering if we've been misinformed about the necessity of wearing our masks or chemical suits. Why are all the soldiers on the court wearing their masks if we don't need to wear ours?

Damn, I'm not thinking clearly. They're just fucking with us. I guess this is our welcome to the desert.

We keep walking.

We enter the airplane hanger. It's been converted into a housing area. There are rows and rows of cots lined up, one cot right next to the other with barely enough room to walk between them.

Most of the cots are occupied with soldiers lying on their new beds. There's really nothing else for them to do. I get a glimpse of my future. Lying on a cot in an airplane hanger.

There are bathrooms outside of the hanger. Wood boxes made into latrines. There are no showers. The food during my stay at this establishment will be dehydrated MREs, meals ready to eat.

I look around for a cot, but I'm not as lucky as the others. All the cots have been taken. I've got a sleeping bag and a hard foam mat.

I could just make do on the floor with the mat and the sleeping bag.

It wouldn't be the first time since I'd joined the Army that I'd found myself sleeping on the floor. But I don't bother with it. It's too hot for a sleeping bag. I'm not sure how temporary these arrangements are, I might need to be ready to go at a moments notice and there might not be enough time for me to put away my sleeping gear.

Yeah, these are all legitimate reasons for not pulling out my sleeping bag, but none of these are the real reasons why I don't want to bother with it.

The real reason? I don't want to be that comfortable.

This is a miserable place and I want to be miserable while I'm here.

The shittier it is here, the better it'll be for me. I don't want to see one ounce of softness or experience one minute of pleasure while I'm here. Comforts like that are only going to remind me of everything I'm missing. It'll remind me of all the things I've left behind and all the things I may never live to see again.

I make myself as uncomfortable as possible on the floor. I use my ruck sack as a pillow. I unbutton my battle dress uniform top and slide it off using it as a blanket. I lie down on the floor wearing my t-shirt and the rest of my uniform and I try not to think about anything at all.

The long flight and the heat must've wore me out more than I realized because I fall asleep lying on the floor.

I get woken up to the screaming sound of a siren. It's loud and long, like a train whistle. I'm so tired, I don't feel completely awake even though my eyes are open.

I have this memory of being young and walking along the train tracks, I don't remember where I was going, probably nowhere, most likely just passing the time.

I felt the ground rumble beneath my feet and then I heard the unmistakable sound of the train whistle. Long and loud, too long and too loud. Next came the clickety-clack sound of the train rolling over the tracks. The train swaying back and forth as each car passed by me.

Clickety-clack . . . . Clickety-clack . . . .

The train lets off one more long whistle before leaving. The train's leaving for good. I feel like it's saying good-bye to me. I wonder. Is it? Is it saying good-bye to me? There will be other trains that come through here on this track, but this particular one will never be here again. This one is gone forever. Just like so many other things in my life.

Gone. Gone forever.

There will always be others, but they'll never be the same. Missed opportunities gone, they're taken off down the tracks to their destination. To their destiny.

My memory gets put on hold when I'm informed the screeching siren is a scud alert. We're told to put on our protective masks.

This clears my head of the dreamy fog I've been in. Of all the things I brought with me and can't seem to find, my mask isn't one of them.

I've had my mask strapped to my side from the moment I left the United States. Along with my rifle, these two things of mine will never get lost. They will be by my side night and day, while I'm sleeping, while I'm using the latrine and eventually if I ever get to shower again they will also be by my side then.

Honestly, my boots are really the only other thing I need to be a soldier. I could toss the rest of this shit in the garbage and I don't think it would matter. I'd be naked. That could be a problem, I guess. I don't know, maybe not. This hanger kind of reminds me of a big circus tent anyway. I seriously doubt anyone would even notice. I imagine the circus themed music playing in my head.

I think I've been lying on this floor for far too long. Maybe it's the heat. Maybe it's just the scud alert that has my thoughts on the crazy side. I take my mask out and secure it tightly to my face.

Then we're told we need to get into all our chemical equipment. Head to toe. Great. With my mask already on my face, I pull out my chemical suit and start putting it on. I put on my chemical jacket and pants. I slip my chemical boots on over my combat boots and then I slide my gloves on. And then?

We wait.

So here I am with my mask on my face and my chemical suit on. I'm covered up from head to toe. I guess we could die tonight. This might be my last moment on the planet. But that's not really my major concern right now.

My concern? I need the latrine. This isn't just any leak either. It's that one you need to take first thing in the morning. The one that feels like it's going to burst out of you at any moment. The one that makes you wonder whether or not you're going to make it all the way to the toilet. The one that feels like it'd last all damn morning when you finally do make it to the bathroom. Yeah. That one.

Damn!

I'm not sure what's bothering me more. The fact that I really gotta go and I can't focus on anything else. Or the fact that taking a leak is all I can focus on during what could very well be the very last moment of my entire life.

Maybe I gotta go so bad it's clouding my thoughts. Damn it anyway. Let this scud alert end so I can piss!!!! Shit. I can't hold it any longer. How am I gona go in the middle of a scud alert? I can't take my suit off now.

I wait.

I try not to think about it. I try not to think about anything at all, and I wait. What else can I do, besides wait? Wait for an all clear signal from the commander so I can take this chemical suit off and use the latrine.

Wait. Wait, wait, wait, wait. I am waiting . . . .

I just have to clear my head. Don't think about anything. Especially not the latrine. Don't think about the latrine. Don't think about water. Or waterfalls, or lakes, or streams. Don't think about any of those things.

We get the all clear signal.

It's all clear. I can take off my mask and my chemical suit and I can finally go to the bathroom.

I'm so relieved. I don't stick around for long. I run outside taking my chemical gloves off while I'm running. I start unbuttoning my pants before I even reach the latrine. Damn? Why did I bother to run all the way to the latrine? I could've just pissed right outside the tent, who would care.

Screw it. I'm already here now.

I'm so relieved I get to relieve myself I don't even bother to take off my mask. I'll do that later. Priorities.

I feel great now. So much better.

I walk out of the latrine and take off my mask as I head back to the hanger. I look around at my new surroundings. This is my new way of life. Living in an airplane hanger, using a wood box for a bathroom, living without showers, eating flop that passes for food, baking in the sun, and being bored out of my skull.

My priorities have definitely changed. As I get used to my new life, I realize my priorities are going to continue to change, depending upon whatever I'll need most at any given moment. Even if that something happens to be using the bathroom. I never expected that using the bathroom was ever going to be at the top of my list of priorities.

I feel the uncertainty of my future snaking itself around me, slowly creeping its way into my life. My uncertain and priority shifting future is a snake I'll be wearing, and one I'll need to quickly get accustomed to. But a snake I'll never get used to.

How can I get used to the possibility that any moment could be my last moment. How can I get used to killing people? How can I get used to watching my back for enemies that present themselves as friends? How can I get used to living like this, in a place so far from my home? I can't. I won't. I will never get used to it, I'll get accustomed to it. And when I leave here, I'll get accustomed to a new way of life.

"You know you can take your chemical suit off." I look around and I realize someone is talking to me. "Your suit. It's all clear. You can take it off." I look at the soldier and I see the rank of Sergeant and I read the name Destino written on the uniform and then I look down at my own uniform and the mask in my hand. "Oh yeah I know, I . . . ." Before I finish talking the other soldier walks away.

I walk back into the circus tent and head for the floor space I've been occupying. Other people here have been calling this place their home. They say their home is wherever they happen to be at the moment. But not me. I don't see it that way. I'll never call this place my home. This is my residence. A home, my home, will be so much more than a place to spend the night.

I lie back down on the floor and I do what we soldiers do best. Wait. We're always waiting for something. Waiting for something to happen and then once it happens, we wait for it to be over. There's only one thing a soldier never waits for, and that's for things to go wrong. Because things will always go wrong. That's the one certainty a soldier will always have. At least there is one thing a soldier can always count on.

Things will always go wrong.

TWO

HANGERS

We wait.

We're getting really good at waiting. I think we've been here for about nine days now, but I'm not really sure. My watch has a calendar on it, but I don't know what I did with my watch, I can't find it. It's just as well. I'm not sure I if want to start counting the days just yet.

I'm still sleeping on the floor. I've gotten kind of accustomed to it. It's not so bad. The bathrooms, I've gotten accustomed to them. The heat? It's not really that bad yet. But then, it's only January. The real heat is on its way, it'll be here soon. I don't have a thermostat, but I don't need one to know that it's hot during the day and it's cold as crazy at night.

I was definitely wrong about it being too hot for a sleeping bag.

I wish I'd known that it gets cold in the desert. I tossed all my cold weather clothes in the trash before I boarded the plane. I didn't think I was going to need it, why carry all that muddle around with me if I'm not going to use it? I thought it was going to be hot here in the desert.

At least I had the good sense to bring along a CD player. Other than walks to the latrine, listening to CDs is the only thing I have to do to pass the time. But this CD player's main function is to drown out the sound of all the idiots I'm stuck here with.

There is always someone running their mouth about some garbage that no one really wants to listen to. I think they talk just to entertain themselves.

Damn it. The batteries in my CD player just died. I know I brought more batteries with me, but hell if I know where they are. Most likely they're in the bottom of my duffle bag along with everything else I can't seem to find. Maybe no one will talk. Maybe everyone will just shut their mouths.

No. No they won't.

Do I really have to listen to this jackass run his mouth? Does he ever shut up? He even talks in his sleep. I hear him telling the others that they might not make it out of here alive and even if they do get out of here alive, they'll probably be missing a few body parts. Who wants to hear this shit? I sure as hell don't want to listen to what this idiot has to say.

I wish he would just shut the fuck up. I wonder if I can knock him unconscious from here if I toss my bayonet at his head. I'm pretty sure I could hit him from here. I wouldn't even have to get up.

Now I know why those bastards were out there on the court playing basketball in their protective masks the day our plane arrived. They where bored out of their minds.

Yes, I think I should toss my bayonet at his head. Where the hell is my bayonet anyway? I look around on the floor, wait no, I slide my hand around my back, here it is. I've got it strapped to my belt.

"Hey soldiers! If you hear your name called, get your gear packed and be ready to go tomorrow morning, you're leaving first thing."

I listen to the jackass read off a list of names, and I'm on it. Yes! I'm finally leaving this hanger and moving on to my unit. I'll be leaving in the morning. One more night of sleeping on the floor. I don't know if that's good or bad, maybe my next location will be even worse.

I find my usual spot on the floor and cover up with my BDU top.

I'm relieved to finally be getting out of this joint. I'm ready to go for a lot of reasons, but one of the more important reasons? It's really starting to stink. All these people crammed up in this circus tent for days without any showers. The heat during the day really intensifies the smell. Hhmmm . . . Maybe that's why those clowns were wearing their protective masks on the basketball court. Maybe they were trying to escape from the smell.

It's an uneventful night and I actually sleep all the way through.

I guess that means I've gotten comfortable. Then this move to a new location is exactly what I need. I don't want to be comfortable.

I don't need to pack anything since I never bothered to unpack anything. As soon as I wake up I'm ready to go. I put on my battle dress uniform top and gather up my ruck sack and duffle bag. I throw my rifle over my shoulder and snap my Kevlar into place. I check my belt to make sure my bayonet is still strapped to my belt. My mask has never left my side. Unless it's on my face, it'll stay securely fastened to my hip at all times.

I walk out of the tent and meet up with the other soldiers who will be leaving the hanger this morning. We're all just standing around waiting for our name to be called off another list so we can be divided up even further. I finally hear the jackass call my name. I am headed to a new location along with one other soldier.

The other soldier and I are handed over to two noncommissioned officers who will be transporting us to our new unit. I don't know if these NCO's are having a bad day, a bad life, or just a bad war because they're acting all pissy pants with us. The other soldier and I seem to be a real inconvenience to them and they let us know it.

The NCO's don't introduce themselves to us and they don't even bother asking us what our names are. They order us to pick up all of our equipment and get in the back of the two and half ton truck. The entire time we're walking the two of them carry on a conversation just between themselves. I hope they weren't trying to hurt my feelings with their childish nonsense because that sure didn't work. I could give a shit what kind of day they're having or what they think about me. I like the crappy mood, I welcome it. I don't want to be comfortable.

The other soldier and I climb aboard the back of the 2 and ½ ton truck, while the two noncommissioned officers climb their fat asses up into the front with their pissy attitudes. Fine by me. These two are better off being as far away from me as possible.

The other soldier and I ride in silence. The back of the vehicle where I'm riding has long narrow benches along each side, I'd prefer the floor, but what the hell, this hard metal bench is pretty uncomfortable so I'll stay sitting on it.

There's a canvas cover stretching out across the top, held up by wood slats and a canvas curtain across the back end. The curtain doesn't close all the way and it flaps in the breeze, sand blows up into the back of the deuce and plasters itself all over our faces. Perfect. I'm feeling less comfortable by the minute. That's the way I like it.

I spend my time staring out the curtain. Sand kicks up immediately behind the vehicle and in the distance all I can see is sand. Smooth sand, drifting sand, sand piles, sand hills, sand roads.

Sand.

After what feels like a 30 minute ride, we stop and we're told to get out.

So we get out.

The pissy pants noncommissioned officers tell us to wait here where we're at. No further instructions. No further information about what the hell's going on or where the hell we're going. No information about what or who we're waiting for. Just wait.

So we wait.

There's nothing but sand here. I turn in a full circle and I see nothing but sun and sand. The deuce filled with the fat-ass NCO's pulls away and leaves a trail of dust behind it as it disappears into the sand. The sound of the engine trails off the further away it moves from me.

My dog tags pick up the brief breeze that blows through and the metal tags clang against one another. A little sand cloud swirls around me and then just as quickly as the breeze came, it leaves and I'm left alone with my thoughts.

Absolute silence.

I've never been anywhere in my entire life that's so peacefully unnerving and disturbingly quiet at the same time. It's difficult to be watchful of an enemy when your surroundings are so relaxing.

I toss my duffle bag into the sand and pull off my ruck sack and turn it into a pillow. Now I don't even get a floor to sleep on. Just sand. Nice. The other soldier takes out a notebook and a pen and starts writing. It's probably a letter home to someone who misses this poor bastard.

That must be difficult to have someone at home missing you like that. Someone to be worried about. Someone to worry about you.

I can't imagine what that must be like. Is it better to have someone care about you? Does it make it easier to get through a debacle like this?

Or does it make it harder to focus on your situation when your attention is divided in two different places? Splitting your focus like that must wear a person out faster. I don't envy this soldier. I prefer it the way I've got it. No one waiting at home for me. All my attention is right here in this very moment.

No distractions and nothing to make me soft. Nothing to make me have the least bit of compassion.

Nothing to do to pass the time. Damn. Writing letters sure would take up a lot of time. Holy shit I am bored. I lie my head back on my ruck sack pillow and cover my face with my BDU hat. I close my eyes and enjoy the silence.

I get woken up by some ass munch kicking me in the legs.

"Well holy hell soldier. Is it nap time? Do you want me to get you a bottle to suck on?"

Did I fall asleep and wake up back in basic training? Who is this asshole?

"Are you kidding me soldier? Are we at the playground? Hey, sugarpants, get your stuff and let's go! I'm not waiting all day for you."

Wasn't I the one who's been waiting all day for this fool? Why am I the one getting bitched at? Whatever. I stand up and I hear, "Hurry the fuck up soldier." So I hurry the fuck up and get I my shit together. The other soldier's already loaded up with two duffle bags, a ruck sack, an M16 rifle and a protective mask.

The other soldier and I look at the asshole who's been bitching at us for the last few minutes and then we give each other a glance. I know I'm thinking, well, what the hell? What's next? Are we gona go, or are we just gona keep . . . .

"Well holy lemons, would you two weaselnuts like your own private invitation? The vehicle's this-a-way. Do you want me get you a baby carriage and push you to the truck in it? You two powder bottoms want to stick around here awhile longer and play on the merry-go-round?"

Nice.

The other soldier and I start walking toward the direction of the ass face's vehicle.

As we walk toward the vehicle, I take the opportunity to survey the asshole's uniform. I look at the front of the uniform and I see the name tag reads Williams and the rank on the collar is a Staff Sergeant. Above the name is a set of airborne wings, an air assault badge and a pathfinder badge. There's a Special Forces tab looming on the upper left sleeve and a combat patch on the right sleeve.

I let out a long sigh and roll my eyes. Great. I really hope this asshole is just my transportation to my new location. I could get along just fine if I never see Sergeant Williams again.

The asshole walks up to a humvee and gets into the driver's seat. The other soldier I'm with starts to get into the passenger's seat to the right of Staff Sergeant Williams.

That was a mistake. I shake my head and think to myself. Here we go.

Sergeant Williams starts barking at the other soldier, "Hey! Hey, hey jingle bells what the hell are doing? Do you seriously think you've earned the right to sit your butter-filled ass in the front seat with me?"

The other soldier looks a little confused. The soldier looks at the front seat and then looks at me. I open the back door of the hummer and nod my head in the direction of the back seat. The soldier stands there, mouth opening in an attempt to talk. I shake my head no and motion again for the back seat.

I climb into the back of the vehicle and the staff sergeant hands me a stack of magazines, each stuffed with 20 rounds of M16 ammunition. I get instructions on what to do in the event we get ambushed. I want to laugh. I want this to be a joke. But it's not.

I try to quickly run through my memory and find the time when I was in basic training and we practiced the proper procedure for a roadside ambush. What was it I'm supposed to do? Get out of the vehicle and find cover in the ditch facing the road, my weapon pointed in the direction we had been traveling? Was that it?

I look out the window at the side of the road. There is no ditch.

I was trained in a forest with cover and concealment. Trees, bushes, ditches and hills. There's nothing but sand here. There's not even a clear distinction between where the road ends and the sand begins. It's just sand. There's really nowhere to find cover.

What the hell? Ahhh . . . Forget it. There's going to be a whole lot of this in my future isn't there? All the training I received is flying out the mother-shitting humvee window, because it just doesn't apply here. I never trained in the desert. But I was trained to make the best of the situation. To make due with what I do have available to me. And what I do have is an M16 and a stack of loaded magazines. That'll do just fine. I can work with that.

The other soldier decides now would be a good time to have a conversation with SSgt. Williams, "Hey, how long have you been here Sergeant?" The other soldier asks towards the front seat.

Williams replies, "Longer than you jingle bells."

"Hey Sergeant, where are we going?"

"You're going wherever I take you. Now shut your sandwich hole."

"Hey Sergeant? Why are you messing with me? I'm getting tired of these games."

"Oh no, I don't think you are soldier. We're just getting started with the fun."

"Hey Sergeant, What's your MOS?"

Damn, this soldier is stupid . . . . Wait, no this clown is too damn slow to be stupid. Why in the hell does this soldier keep talking to Sergeant Williams? Who gives a flying crap what military occupational specialty the sergeant has? I do not care what kind of job SSgt. Williams has. Pain in the ass is this Sergeant's job.

"Hey Sergeant! It's my birthday today. Did you know that?"

"Is that right soldier? I got a little birthday present for you."

SSgt. Williams reaches back toward the other soldier and hands the soldier a stack of loaded magazines.

"Happy fucking birthday soldier!"

The soldier looks them over and loads one magazine into the M16 rifle and lets the other magazines find their home in some BDU pockets. "Hey Sergeant, when's your birthday?"

"September 31st."

"September 31st? Oh no kidding huh? That's a ways off, ain't it, Sergeant?"

SSgt. Williams pulls up to a security check point and stops the vehicle. There's a pretty lengthy conversation transpiring between Sergeant Williams and the guards at the check point. I can't really hear anything they're saying, but I see SSgt. Williams make a few nods in the direction of myself and the other soldier as the guards look us over. What are they saying? Is it good? Is it bad? Damn, I don't know. I don't want to know.

Sergeant Williams pulls the hummer forward past the guards and into the unit's perimeter and parks the vehicle next to a tent. We all get out of the vehicle and I look around at my surroundings.

Tents, generators, military vehicles, sun and sand. The tents look so haphazard, assembled in no particular pattern. They're just randomly spread throughout the area. Some tents are close to others and then there's a few smaller ones set farther away from the rest of the tents. There are humvees and deuce and half trucks parked right up next to the individual tents.

Most of the tents have generators right next to them. The bigger the tent, the bigger the generator. The bigger tents have generators set up on the back of trailers and the smaller tents have little ones sitting in the sand next to their respective tents.

This looks like a damn tent trailer park. The only thing it's missing is laundry hanging out on the line to dry. Oh no, wait. There is laundry hanging off the sides of the tents.

There are two wood boxes set off far away from the tents. Latrines? One of the boxes has a large round container sitting on the top of it and it's connected to a generator. That can't be a latrine. What the hell is it then? Is it? Could it be? It's a shower. Holy shit! It's a shower! It's been almost two weeks since my last shower.

"Hey soldier you can sight-see and buy post-cards later, let's go."

I follow Sergeant Williams and I'm led into one of the trailer park tents. I'm introduced to Sgt. Evers. Sgt. Fat-Ass is more like it. SSgt. Williams leaves the tent and I feel a moment of victory. I am free of Staff Sergeant Williams!

I'm silently enjoying my victory when I hear Sgt. Evers running down the rules of the tent. This lecture is going to go on for awhile. Damn. I just exchanged one asshole for another one.

I could really go for a drink right now. An ice cold bottle of beer. Maybe a shot of whiskey? No. No, no. Definitely the ice cold bottle of beer, because it's hotter than a sandy beach in Alaska in here and then once I finish the beer I could chuck the empty bottle at Sgt. Evers.

I listen to Sgt. Evers ramble on. Actually, I'm not listening at all.

I just try to look serious and give an occasional nod. I walk towards an empty cot that's at the opposite end of the tent from Sgt. Evers' mouth. I toss my rucksack down into the sand next to the cot and I take my duffle bag off my back and throw it down next to my rucksack.

At least this tent isn't ripe the way the old circus tent was. It doesn't smell like anything in this tent. It's just hot. I look over in the direction of Sgt. Evers. Wow. Still talking. I give another nod and pretend to be interested in all these tent rules I'm suppose to be learning.

I unhook my water canteen from my belt and I start empting the canteen into my mouth. I'm sweating like a lemon in the sun. I think about sitting down on the cot, but it's way too hot in here, I've got to get out of this tent.

I tell Sgt. Evers I'm going to fill up my canteen and head for the tent door. I get myself a whole two steps outside the door and I hear, "Well holy hell soldier. Where in the world do you think you're sneaking off to?"

The words slap me in the back of the head. Shit, I thought I was free of Staff Sergeant Williams. That's just great!

I hold up my empty canteen and shake it.

"Soldier are you telling me that you're walking around in the desert with an empty canteen? Is that what you're telling me? 'Cause that's what I'm hearing. I don't believe my fucking ears. Alright soldier, let's go. I'll take your ass to the water buffalo"

Water buffalo?

SSgt. Williams walks through the tent trailer park and I trail behind. We stop in front of a sand colored water tank with the words 'potable water' stamped across the side. Not exactly a kitchen sink, and not exactly how I pictured a water buffalo, but it's water. I turn on the tap and I fill up my canteen with water that's been baking in this tank all day. I take a drink and the water is coffee pot hot and tastes like bleach.

"Soldier, if you are all finished drinking your tea, let's go."

Do I even want to know where I am going now? I don't, no I really don't. We walk through the trailer park and stop in front of a small sand pit. There are two soldiers with shovels, they're busy making the pit even bigger.

"Soldier! Soldier, what are you waiting on soldier, pick up a shovel. Damn, you jokers dig slower than shit. This foxhole doesn't look any bigger than it was when I left this morning."

I listen to SSgt. Williams while I pick up a shovel and join the other soldiers in the soon-to-be foxhole and I start digging.

"Alright turds I'll be back later to check on your slow-ass progress. You're gona be here until it's finished."

SSgt. Williams walks away and I go back to digging a hole in the sand. The other soldiers stop digging as soon as Williams is out of sight. Specialist Leon and Sergeant Destino introduce themselves to me. I recall Sgt. Destino from the airplane hanger, telling me I could take off my chemical suit. I never get around to asking what the Sergeant was doing at the hanger.

Specialist Leon lights up a cigarette and offers one to Sgt. Destino who declines the offer. Spec. Leon offers me one and I take it. I'm not a smoker, but at the moment smoking a cigarette seems like a better alternative to digging a hole in the sand.

I ask if Sergeant Williams is always such an asshole. Specialist Leon and Sergeant Destino both exchange looks and laugh.

THREE

SMOTSS

Here we are. Here I am. I'm sitting here waiting again. I'm waiting for Specialist Leon who went to talk to some lieutenant at this military police camp.

We're here to get directions to the Army field hospital. We're going to pick up Sergeant Russell, he was in a fight with a couple of Iraqis and he got stabbed in the leg. He's being released from the hospital today and sent back to our unit.

His injury only happened 3 days ago, so I guess that's good, his leg must not be that bad, at least it's not bad enough for him to be sent home anyway. Is that good or bad? I guess that all depends on a person's perspective. It's good, his leg isn't all jacked up. It's bad, because he's gotta come back to this mess and keep fighting.

Usually when a soldier gets injured, injured bad enough anyway, they get sent to the Army field hospital and then shipped off to Germany. Once they get to Germany they eventually get sent back home to the United States.

If you ask me, it's not worth it. I'd rather stay here and do my time instead of getting an early release back home and suffer through an injury. Not everyone heals from their injuries, not everyone survives their injuries.

I don't think much of Sergeant Russell. I don't think much of him because he didn't really get stabbed in the leg. I know what really happened.

I heard him talking about getting out of here and going back home. He said couldn't take it anymore. He stabbed himself in the leg with his own bayonet. He said he could get out of here and no one would know that his injury was self-inflicted.

He's blaming that shit on some Iraqis and now when he finally does go home he'll probably leave here with a couple of medals for being a hero.

That's bullshit.

We all want to get out of here. But that isn't the way to do it. That's a fucking coward. Russell is a fucking coward. A coward that I don't want to drive across the desert to pick up. But I don't get choices in the Army. So I will drive across the desert to pick up this motherfucker and take him back to our unit.

It's still bullshit though.

How long does it take to get directions anyway? I've been waiting here in this deuce for almost 20 minutes already. He's talking, I know he is. Specialist Leon can talk forever.

He talks about nothing, but people listen anyway because he makes the shit sound so interesting that you just can't help yourself. You want to hear what he has to say.

I let out a long sigh and take a look around at my surroundings.

Over to the right and a little in front of me is the military police camp where Leon is burning a hole in someone's ear right now. It looks a lot like every other military unit's desert set-up. Tents and generators sprawled out haphazardly across the sand.

Directly in front of me sits a line of sand-colored military vehicles.

A convoy of military vehicles headed to their new location has made a stop here. The drivers and passengers are lingering inside and out of the vehicles waiting for further instructions. They have their weapons slung across their backs, water canteens in their dirty sand-colored hands.

Behind me are the remains of dead bodies, destroyed Iraqi vehicles, tanks, bunkers and military equipment. Everything's still burning from the bombs that have been dropped. Shit that's all been destroyed by the friendly forces.

Immediately to my right, are the friendly landmines, buried beneath the sand by the friendly forces. Friendly forces being us. Us, being the U.S. Us.?? U.S.? That's funny.

To my left are the unfriendly landmines, placed there by the enemy. The enemy being, Iraq. I. Raq. The enemy is I. Raq. I. Raq is fighting U.S. I think it's the heat. It makes me find things amusing that aren't amusing at all.

Beyond the friendly landmines are the Kuwaiti oil fires, there's a lot of them burning. Today the wind is blowing west and it's blowing all the smoke with it, so the sky directly above me is black from the oil fires.

Shit . . . . I'm hungry.

Leon isn't going to be back for awhile, not the way he talks.

I wonder if there are any MREs in here. I hate eating these puke tasting dehydrated meals ready to eat. There is nothing about these pieces of crap that are ready to be eaten. I find an MRE stuffed under the driver's seat.

Ham Slice.

I open it. I smell it. Maybe I'll just drink water. I'm not that hungry. Yes I am. Alright, stomach here come the groceries. I take a bite of the ham. Ham? Really? I don't think this is ham at all. Ugh, this ham is nasty. I wish I wasn't so hungry.

I eat my ham and enjoy the view, to my left, just beyond the unfriendly landmines sit a shitload of Iraqi bunkers, dug deep into the sand.

I watch as several American soldiers venture out past the landmines. They're rummaging through the bunkers, walking down into them and through them.

I've been inside a few Iraqi bunkers and I was impressed at how elaborate they are. They're intricate, like an underground subway, with tunnels and rooms, doors and furniture.

I watch as the soldiers walk past the second row of bunkers. There are about six or seven soldiers walking side by side. They're loaded up with M16's, 9mm's, flame-throwers, grenades, rocket launchers, a couple of 60 cal's and one 50 caliber weapon.

I take another bite of my ham and I hear gun fire. I look up to see the American soldiers advancing on the bunkers. There are Iraqis inside the second row of bunkers and they've started firing at the soldiers.

These stupid MP's!! They've been sitting here at this site for over four days now and they didn't know there were Iraqis in the bunkers!!

As soon as others realize what's happening they're quick to grab whatever weapons they have available. Some soldiers are driving humvees, some are on foot, everyone's headed to the bunkers like ants swarming over an ant hill. I reach for my loaded M16 rifle and start to get out of the deuce and a half.

I hear the distinct tat-tat-tat of M60 automatics firing and I see the flame thrower destroying up the bunkers. The M16 rifles are pissing bullets at the enemy.

I hear a loud bang against the side of my door. I look out to see Specialist Leon. "Get out here, take SMOTSS with you and head over to the front of the convoy."

"What the hell is a SMOTSS?"

"It's not a what it's a who?"

"Well, who is he?"

"Damn! SMOTSS, is not a he, he is a SHE! Now take her with you and head to the front of the convey! Get behind the front vehicles, they're gona need cover on the bunkers!"

I see a soldier running up behind Leon, this must be SMOTSS. I look her over and I see a blood covered bayonet, a 60 cal strapped across her back, she's carrying her locked and loaded M16 in her hands, grenades dangling from her ammo belt and she's wearing the meanest look I've ever seen a soldier wear.

We take off together towards the front of the convoy and settle behind the lead vehicle of the convoy to observe our field of fire. I raise my M16, take off the safety and I chamber a round, I stretch out my left arm and let the front of the barrel rest in my sand-colored hand. My dirt-covered right hand settles at the back of the rifle, I curl my trigger finger through the tiny loop and let it rest next to the trigger, I pull the rifle close against my right shoulder and I close my left eye, tilt my head slightly and line up the front and rear sights.

I have an Iraqi in my sights and as I pull my finger around the trigger, he falls to the ground before I follow through on the trigger.

SMOTSS.

Damn, she's fast with the trigger finger.

"What does SMOTSS mean anyway?"

"Saint Michaela of the South Side."

"South side of what?"

Three Iraqis make their way out of the bunker and start running full force straight towards our location. SMOTSS and I start firing our M16s at the oncoming Iraqis, two of them fall to sand, but the third one keeps running straight for us.

SMOTSS picks up her M60 and swings it around ass-backwards and thrusts the butt-end of it straight into the Iraqi's face. The third Iraqi gets his turn to fall to the sand like the other two.

Blood leaks out of the Iraqi's head and stains the sand around him, turning it dark. I hear him gasp for air as he chokes on the blood pouring down the back of his throat and filling his lungs, he gargles the blood like mouthwash.

SMOTSS and I do a quick search across his dead body, relieving him of his weapons and ammunition.

He's not wearing a uniform. They're just regular, everyday clothes. He doesn't have combat boots either. He's wearing flip-flops. How can you fight the enemy in a get-up like that?

I'm not sure why I expected him to look like me. But he doesn't. I'm relieved. I don't want this cocksucker to look like me. He should look like what he is. An enemy. A dead enemy.

Fuck him! I'm not going to feel sorry for this piece of shit, I'm not going to feel anything for this enemy. How many American soldiers did this dead Iraqi kill? How many American soldiers did he slice apart with his booby-traps and landmines?

The flame-thrower makes its final sweep through the bunkers. If there were any Iraqi's left in those bunkers, they're done now. Set on fire by the flame-thrower.

They have to clear the bunkers, something the MP's should have done when they first got here, but they didn't. If the Iraqi's don't come out, the flame-thrower will solve that problem melting their skin with flames of fire.

I see the remaining Iraqis surrounded by American soldiers. Moments ago they were armed soldiers, fighting against the American soldiers and now here they are captured, defenseless enemy prisoners of war.

I turn around and SMOTSS is gone. Alright, well nice working with you.

I head back to the two and half ton truck Leon and I have been driving. I climb back inside on the passenger's side and do what a soldier does best. I wait.

I look over to my right at the Kuwaiti oil fires, the black smoke looming above my head, the miles and miles and miles of sand, I think of the landmines buried beneath the sand, the burning vehicles and the dead bodies behind me, and I let out another long sigh and I go back to eating my MRE.

Specialist Leon hops into the driver's seat and we take off for the hospital. There isn't much to look at during the ride. There's sand, and lots of it.

We drive through the sand for about 40 minutes and that's when I see a huge white tent sitting in the middle of the desert. It's the hospital where Sgt. Russell has been.

The sides of the white tent aren't tied down well and the bottom of the tent flaps around, clanging against the metal poles. Tiny little sand tornados swirl around the bottom edges of the tent, the wind blowing the sand wherever it demands.

I open my door and climb out, stepping on the make-shift steps. I snap my Kevlar helmet in place, throw my rifle over my shoulder and check to make sure I have all my equipment with me. Canteen, bayonet, protective mask, chemical suit, ammunition. I'm a little short on ammunition. I'll have to take care of that when I get back to the unit.

Carrying all this equipment around was heavy the first few days, but it's not heavy anymore. It is wet though. Especially my uniform. The sun is so intense, I sweat from the time the sun rises until it sets.

All the sweat makes my uniform stick to me and the parts of my body that aren't covered with clothing, my hands and face, are covered with sand. All that sweat makes it easy for the sand to stick to me.

We trudge through the sand, my boots sink in with each step. I pull my foot out of the sand and take a new step. Into the sand my boot goes. Step. Sink. Pull. Step. Sink. Pull. On and on the process repeats itself everywhere I walk in this desert.

We approach the entrance to the white hospital tent. The wind picks up and I hear the bottom edges of the tent flapping against itself, the sand kicks up and swirls around.

The inside of the tent is air conditioned. It feels like . . . . What exactly does it feel like in here? The relief from the heat is so amazing I can't find the words to describe how the cool air feels against my heat soaked skin.

All the sweat that had been piling up on my skin begins to evaporate and I start to get a little cold. Cold. I'm actually cold.

These lucky bastards. I should have been a medic. I could be sitting inside this air conditioned tent all day instead of roasting out in the heat. Why should these doctors get to sit inside with the air conditioning? Alright, well, I guess if someone is a heat casualty, I guess they need to be inside with the cool air blowing on them.

But, damit! I want to spend all day in the AC. I want to be a medic. Bastards.

We walk through the mysterious white corridors past rows of soldiers lying on white hospital cots. None of the soldiers are moving, they all lie still.

Everything is white. The tent walls, the blankets covering the soldiers, the bandages covering their wounds, everything. White. There's a thin white layer of material stretched out across the ground, making a white floor.

The only noise in here is the steady hum of the air conditioner.

Leon and I walk up to a woman dressed in white and he questions her on the where abouts of Sgt. Russell. "Are you a doctor?"

"I'm a nurse, honey."

Leon tries to stifle a smile. I think he enjoys being referred to as honey.

"Really?"

"Whatcha looking for?"

"Well, I'm. I'm looking for a. Looking for. I'm trying to uh, I'm trying to find Sergeant Russell. He was brought here with a. A, um."

Are you kidding me Leon. "A leg injury."

"Yeah, a leg. I mean a leg injury, a few days ago."

The nurse flips through some paperwork sitting on the desk behind her.

Leon looks at me and smiles. He strands up straighter. What is he doing? Is he trying to look taller? I roll my eyes and look away from the spectacle unfolding in front of me.

"Hhmmm . . . Hmm, hmm. Yep. He's gone. He left early this morning for Germany."

Gone? Gone! That bastard is gone! He's going to get to go home with his bullshit story and a shitload of medals stuck to his chest and someone like SMOTSS will never see a medal in her life.

That's bullshit.

We walk out of the white tent into the heat and back to our deuce.

Step. Sink. Pull.

Leon looks at me while his boots fight the on-going battle with the sand. "That was some crazy shit, huh?"

"I know. Germany, can you believe Sgt. Russell is gone?"

"Oh, yeah sure. That too, but I meant the nurse? Did you see that shit? She was all over me."

"What?"

"Yeah, I mean, she was a little over the top wasn't she? Shit. She wants this."

Leon slides his dirty hand through his hair, smoothing out his sand-filled high and tight and puts his sun glasses on his dirt covered face.

He really thinks he's something doesn't he? Even with all that sand plastered to his face and hands, the dirty matted hair, the scuffed up boots and his dirty sand covered uniform. When he smiles you can see where the sand has stuck to his teeth and has become just plain old mud. I wonder if he knows he stinks? Neither one of us has showered in over four days and he thinks he's really something right now. Well, it's good to have confidence.

"Smoke?"

"Alright, why not." I take one of the cigarettes Leon offers me, I slide the tip into my mouth and search for my lighter. I light up and inhale deeply feeling the dark smoke fill my lungs as we sit on the hood of the truck. Neither one of us is in any hurry to return to our unit.

What for?

We have our freedom at the moment and as soon as we get back to our unit there's going be some new bullshit waiting for us.

These brief moments of freedom are in short supply. A moment away from supervisors, a moment away from the enemy, a moment away from stupid details and rules that don't seem to make any sense. A brief moment away from the war.

I slowly inhale the smoke, lean back on the hood of the deuce and watch the wind blow the sand where ever it chooses and I feel the heat of the sun pound down around us.

In moments like this I can imagine that I'm not in Iraq. I can imagine that I'm back home hanging out with an old friend. These moments are so brief and I want to make them last, I want to stretch them out for as long as I can because these are the moments that get me through this mess. These are the moments that keep me sane.

FOUR

STRAWBERRIES

I start to get accustomed to my life in the desert. It could be worse. Couldn't it?

I've been here for 36 days. 36 days in the desert. 36 days in a war and I'm still alive. So it could definitely be worse. I've got that going for me, I guess.

I have 144 days left to go here before I get to go back home. That's too many days, so I'm just going to keep counting the number of days I've already been here until I get to the half-way point. Then I'll start counting the number of days I have left.

I get to hear SSgt. Williams run that mouth everyday. So, you know, that's something to look forward to.

Not a day goes by that I don't get bit by some torturous bug of some sort. Those insects come out at night and sneak up on me, I have no defense when I'm asleep. Every morning I wake up with a new bug bite. I guess that's something else to look forward to.

Some soldiers here have big green mosquito nets that they hang over the top of their cots to keep the bugs away at night. I should really get one of those.

I've been eating meals ready to eat for 36 days. After 36 days, dehydrated MREs don't really taste so bad, plus when I eat this shit I pretend I'm an astronaut, so you know, one more thing to look forward to. The chicken with rice MRE is actually edible, it's a favorite of mine. I look forward to getting that one.

There's an oatmeal cookie bar in one of the meals ready to eat that tastes exactly like sandpaper. How do I know what sandpaper tastes like? For the same reason I know what mud, worms, spoiled milk and lake water tastes like.

Anyone who's ever had an older brother will know exactly what all that stuff tastes like too. If you've ever had the kind of brother you just never stop pointing at, you'll know. I look forward to never getting the oatmeal cookie bar.

Our unit is moving to a new location later today. We're moving closer to the Saudi Arabian, Iraqi border. I never get a lot of information about where we're going or why. I just get a lot of information on what to do, when to do it and how to do it. Never why.

We've spent the morning tearing down our entire area. We've torn down just about all the tents. There's just Colonel Bahanda's tent left to tear down. That'll be the last thing we take down, just before we leave.

After all the tents are disassembled they're loaded onto the back of the deuce and half trucks along with all the tent poles and generators. One piece at a time everything gets put on the back of the vehicles.

Even the latrine and the shower get loaded up, otherwise we'd be without them. It's not like there's going to be any bathroom and shower facilities waiting for us at our new location. It's just going to be another nowhere place in the middle of the sand.

Everything we had inside our tent gets packed up too. All the laundry that was hanging out on the tent ropes to dry gets folded up and put away. The water buffalo gets connected to the back of a deuce. All the bigger generators sitting on trailers get connected to a deuce.

The extra weapons and ammunition get the VIP treatment. They're behind the velvet ropes and the bouncers. They get loaded onto one very specific truck, one that will never be used for anything else.

The truck's sole purpose in life is to transport its precious cargo of weapons from one place to another. It travels in its own convey, with armed guards inside and out. One humvee in front with a M60 automatic weapon and a gunner secured to the center of the roof. One identical twin hummer in the rear with the same M60 and matching gunner.

The VIP convoy has already left our current location.

There is also an advance team of soldiers who have already left earlier this morning. They're called the quartering party.

I think that's a misleading term. Because what they're doing isn't really much of a party at all.

They are the ones who arrive first at our new location. They are the ones responsible for setting the stage for us to follow. They clear the way for the rest of us, they find any enemies who might be in that location waiting to ambush us. They will certainly be the first to know if there have been any landmines left behind or if there have been any chemicals used in the area. They clear the path of obstacles that may hinder the movement of the upcoming convoy.

When I think about a party, none of that shit comes to mind. That's a party I don't want an invitation to. But I'll get my invitation eventually, whether I want it or not because I don't get choices in the Army and I don't get to decline party invitations.

I hope this quartering party does a better job of clearing the area than those MPs did at that site Leon and I were at last week when we were getting directions to the hospital.

It's already eleven, tearing down all this equipment would go a whole lot faster if the officers ever got off their asses and actually worked. But they're too good for that. They let us handle the real work and it's just as well, because they'd dick it up anyway and then we'd be stuck having to do it all over again. You know, by the end of this war I'm going to figure out the purpose of an officer.

We finally tear down Colonel Bahanda's tent and load it onto a humvee. The last of the foxholes we dug earlier have been filled back in and covered up. All the vehicles have been lined up in a single file row. When we leave this location there won't be anything left behind, not a single clue left behind for anyone to discover that we were ever here.

Now there's just one thing left to do before we leave.

Wait.

I am always waiting. When I finally get out of this shit hole and back to the States, I wonder if I should put waiting on my job application as one of the valuable skills I acquired in the Army? I mean, why not. I'm really good at it. Actually, that's not true at all. I'm not good at it, I suck at it. I hate waiting. It's so damn boring.

Dammit.

I wish I had someone back home to write a letter to, that would occupy my time. But what would I even say in a letter. I've got nothing to write about.

Dear Loved One, I am so bored. All we ever do here is sit around and wait. I'm going to send you this letter now and then I'm going to wait for you to write back to me.

Ah . . . Forget writing. I'm glad I don't have anyone to write to. It's better this way. No reason to subject anyone to this brutal boredom.

Boredom.

I should have brought a book with me. Because a book is more than just something to read. If it's done right, a book could take me out of this desert and off to a new location. A book can take me anywhere the writer wants me to go.

Finally. We are getting the hell out of here. The 1st Sergeant calls all of us over so we can receive our safety briefing. Yeah, really. That's important, we need that. You know, because after all we're in the middle of a war, so we probably weren't aware that we should be careful and shit.

You know, yeah, that's good. Great, thanks for letting me know to be on the look out for the enemy who will be carrying a rifle. Because, yeah, I didn't know that.

Yes, I certainly will put my Kevlar helmet on my head before we drive away because that's gona protect me from . . . ???? What exactly?

This isn't a damn construction site, there isn't any chance of someone dropping a bucket of nails on my head, I'm not going to get hit in the head with a 2x4. I'm just going to get shot with a rifle, or step on a land mine. What's this stupid helmet going to do for me then? Not a damn thing.

I get stuck driving a deuce. It's not a horrible vehicle, but it's so big and loud. The engine is so loud I can't hear myself complaining in my own head.

My assistant driver is no stack of pancakes. This guy is so bitchy. I've never heard anyone complain so much in my life. He's going to make someone an excellent wife someday.

We're headed to a new location that's closer to Iraq. Apparently I've been in Saudi Arabia this whole time. Anyway, I'm told it's about a four hour drive to our new location.

I wait. Yes that's right, I WAIT! Wait for the lead vehicle to take off so we can get this pissing convoy moving.

We're going to move to a new location and start the haphazard set-up all over again.

What? Why the hell is Sgt. Pancakes trying to talk to me? I don't want to talk to this clown. Shit! Shut up already. I just want to drive. I wish this trip was longer than four hours because when we get to the new location we're going to be working our asses off setting everything up again.

Shut up Pancakes.

I pull out the throttle knob on the dashboard and it makes the engine idle higher and louder, I'm hoping this will completing drown out the blabbering Pancake I'm forced to listen to.

Drive. Drive. Drive. Follow the truck in front of me. Shit it's hot in here and the sound of this engine is putting me to sleep.

There's nothing but sand and the convoy in front of me to look at. My eyelids start to weigh heavier than my duffle bag. How can I possibly keep my eyes open any longer? I'll just close one eye at a time. Let one eye rest and then let the other one rest. I'm not sure, but I think I might have had both of my eyes closed for a second there.

No harm done. This convoy isn't stopping anywhere for another three hours anyway. I wonder if I could actually sleep while I'm driving?

Oh damn. When did my head get so heavy? I think my head weighs as much as two duffle bags, easily. Maybe even three duffle bags. I can't keep my head held up straight anymore, it's so heavy. My eyelids struggle to stay open and my head wiggles around like a fishing bobber sitting on a lake. Up and down, left and right, round and round. I think I'm drooling on myself.

Oh hell! Hell, was I just snoring? I look over at Pancakes and I see his mouth moving. What? Is he actually talking to me? I can't hear a shitting thing he's saying, the engine is way too loud. Good. Then there's no way he heard me snoring, if I was. I'm not sure if I was, I might have been.

I was definitely drooling though, I use the back of my hand to wipe away the drool on my lower lip and across my chin. I get the drool but leave a smudge of sand across my face in the process from my dirty, sand-covered hand.

The steady hum of the engine and the heat are brutal to my ability to stay awake.

What is that? Am I seeing things?

I see a small Iraqi tent community just sitting out in the middle of nowhere.

I blink my eyes several times in an attempt to wake them up and shake off the heaviness of sleep that's been attacking me for the past hour.

Tents. I see tents. I actually see something other than the vehicle in front of me and the sand I've been staring at for so long.

All the tents together are basically a city, but there aren't any actual structures, it's all tents. A city of tents. And they're not even good tents, they're raggedy tents, they're falling apart and they don't have all the sides to them and what is there isn't tied down very well.

Are those goats inside the tents? Why the world would anyone have goats inside their tent?

There are several small children that start running up to the truck as we drive past, they're swarming around us from every angle. They run out in front of my path and they try climbing on the sides of the truck.

My assistant driver, Sergeant Pancakes starts yelling at me not to stop. Pancakes is warning me that just because they're children doesn't mean they're not dangerous. They are still the enemy, just smaller versions. They may be dangerous, and they will no doubt attempt to kill us just the same way any adult enemy would.

I begin to slow down so I don't hit any of the children. They're swarming around us. The slower I go the louder Pancakes yells at me. I'm thinking in my mind that they're harmless, innocent children and if I don't slow down I might hit one of them.

I make my thoughts known and Pancakes makes it clear that speeding up is not a suggestion, it's an order. He tells me not to worry about the little bastards who are too stupid to get out of the way. I say they're not stupid, they're hungry and they're just children.

I speed up and I try not to look at the children. The faster I drive the faster my heart races with the fear that I may run them over, and I feel guilty for not feeding them.

What am I suppose to do? Follow an order and leave these hungry children on the side of the road? Do I disobey an order and stop, knowing full well the rest of this convey isn't going to stop and we'll be left behind.

What if Pancakes is right, what if this is a trap? What if these children are just a decoy, set up to stop us, so the enemy can kill us? Except for the fact that Pancakes and I are not anyone important, why would anyone bother to kill us? Maybe they don't know we're not important. Maybe they think we're useful and important.

I hear children screaming as I drive forward. I hear them scream louder as the truck lurches forward. I reach down beside my feet where I find the leftovers from my MRE's.

It's all the shit I don't want to eat. I have a bag full of dehydrated strawberries. The only fruit I've had since I got here. These MRE strawberries taste like vomit, unless you're really hungry and then they're delicious. I'm not that hungry yet, but these children seem to be. I start to toss the MRE strawberries out the window to the children.

The children snatch them up. They instantly start jumping off the truck they had just been so desperately clinging to. They're not sure what it is yet, but they all want some of it. I can see them in my side mirror as I drive away.

I wonder if they know you're supposed to add water to the strawberries first before you eat them? I guess not. They're all tearing into the packages and they're devouring the strawberries.

I smile and I look over at my assistant driver, who has a blank look on his face that quickly turns to irritation. Pancakes tells me I'm an asshole. Yeah, well alright. Thanks for that little bit of information. I could do without hearing that. My smile fades and I go back to focusing on the road. Road did I say road? I meant sand path. I go back to focusing on the sand path in front of me.

I keep driving and follow along in the convoy.

I don't know how anyone knows where they're going in this desert. I'm glad I'm not leading this convoy. I'd get lost for sure. There's nothing but sand here and it all looks the same. There's no landmarks to guide your way through the desert.

I'm not sure if it's my imagination, but I think these sand hills move. One day they're on one side of the road and the next day they've moved to the other side of the road. Is that possible? Is it the wind moving the sand across the street or is it just my imagination?

Here we are, we arrive at our new location. I park the deuce and a half in a spot that's been designated by the quartering party. I am in no hurry to get out of my vehicle because I know exactly what I'm going to be doing as soon as I get out.

I'm going to wait.

After I'm all done waiting, I'm going to be working my ass off with the process of setting up all the equipment we tore down earlier in the day. A process I start to get the hang of. I understand the order of things. The order of rank, of which I have none.

We start with the tent of the highest ranking officer in the unit. My tent will be the last one to get set up. We have to make sure the officers don't actually do any work. What a bunch of goofs. How can you possibly feel good about yourself as a person, as a man, when you stand back at let someone else do your work for you?

I wish I could call in sick today. I want to spend the day lying on my couch watching TV and stuffing food in my mouth until I fall asleep.

I want to walk to the refrigerator and pull out an ice cold beer.

I want something insignificant to complain about, like sitting in my air conditioned car and complaining about the traffic while I drive across the paved highway to my shitty insignificant job instead of being here in this oven, dodging bullets.

Hell. Let me get started, the sooner I get started the sooner I can finish and go to sleep.

Nobody here wants to hear my complaints anyway. I should just be grateful that I'm still alive instead of bitching about shit that doesn't even matter.

I need to remind myself I'm a soldier.

That wishing and wanting bullshit is weak. I am a soldier.

Let me do the job I was sent here to do.

With the heat pounding down on me I walk over to the row of two and a half ton trucks and I begin the process of unloading the equipment and setting up the unit, one tent pole at a time.

FIVE

DETAILS

It's hot.

It's seriously hot. I think it's about 115 degrees. I don't know where it's hotter, outside or inside the tent. Outside, there is no shade and I'm directly in the sun and there is no breeze, but somehow the air feels lighter outside the tent. I decide to go inside, because at least there's shade, but inside, the air feels heavy as I breathe it in.

This tent is a disaster. Everyone has their own sleeping cot and each one is surrounded with so much stuff. Duffle bags, ruck sacks, boots, water bottles and uniforms piled up underneath, on top of and next to the cots. Some soldiers have stashes of food under their cots, food that arrived in the form of gifts sent from home.

I know the food sent from home is intended as a nice gesture, but the people at home just don't know how fast chocolate melts in the desert, they don't know that the smell of tuna fish in this heat is disgusting. It never seems to occur to the people at home to send along a can opener with the canned food they send.

I'm sure the people at home mean well.

There are big yellow plastic tubs tipped over and strewn across the floor, they are used for hand washing laundry. The floor of the tent is just the ground that was already here before we set up the tent. A big sand floor that keeps everything in here dirty.

There's laundry hung up to dry above the cots, wet clothes and uniforms are tossed over the black electric lighting cords. At the end of the cords a single light bulb dangles and swings back and forth.

This tent happens to have two light bulbs. That's it, two light bulbs to light up an entire tent that is occupied by a dozen soldiers. Although I'm not sure it really matters because it's bright enough during daylight hours so we don't need lights during the day. We have one of the nicer tents that has screens so we can roll up the heavy canvas sides of the tent and let light and air in through the screens.

At night we have to obey the light and noise discipline rule so the sides of the tent have to be rolled back down, making the inside of the tent dark and the air inside heavy. If you happen to come in to the tent late at night because you've actually been working, the lights will already be off. I made the mistake of turning on the lights during one of those late night work occasions and everyone in my tent got all bent out of shape about it.

I couldn't believe it really. It's two tiny little light bulbs that barely light up anything, not only that, if you're tired enough you can sleep through just about anything. So maybe the people in my tent need to work harder then the light won't bother them at night. I've just used my flashlight ever since that late night incident.

I spend most of my days sweating and drinking water. I lie down on my cot and I try to move as little as possible, I'll sweat less that way.

I hear Sergeant Evers mouth start to run wanting to know why I don't ever get any mail. Don't I have anyone waiting at home for me? Don't I ever write to anybody, doesn't anybody ever write to me? I tell Sgt. Evers to piss off and I immediately wish I hadn't, because it took way too much energy to speak.

My brown cotton t-shirt is soggy from all the sweat. My chocolate chip cookie colored uniform pants are heavy with sweat and gravity is constantly tugging them toward the ground. I've lost a few pounds since I've been here so none of my clothes fit as snug as they used to.

That extra looseness in the pants is causing a constant rub of big wet clothes on a hot sweaty body and it's making my midsection raw. I tighten up my belt, that should help the situation some.

I hear Evers' mouth running on and on about nothing important, I try to tune out the sound and pretend it doesn't exist. Shut up, just shut up.

Why can't these people just shut the hell up. Can't these assholes ever stop running their mouths. I need to tune them out and just ignore them before they irritate me anymore. It's too hot to listen to people talking, the hotter it gets the more annoying their voices become.

These clowns don't have anything else to do but annoy other people. I really don't want to hear their mouths anymore.

Can't I just sweat in peace?

My feet feel heavy and swollen. I should take off these black and green leather jungle boots and change my socks. I know my feet have already sweat through my black wool socks and if I don't change them soon I'm going to get more blisters across the bottom of my soles.

I'm spared being forced to listen to any more shit spewing from Sgt. Evers' mouth when Specialist Leon barrels into the tent. "What are you doing?"

"Nothing. Sweating."

"Yeah, who ain't? Aw shit, y'awl got a cooler in here?"

Leon bounces over to the big orange and white cooler sitting in the middle of the tent and fishes out a bottle of lemonade.

"I wouldn't drink that if I were you Leon."

"No, why not, what the hell it's lemonade ain't it?"

Leon twists off the lid and raises the bottle to his mouth, he tilts his head back for a huge guzzle, not just a sip.

"Leon, don't drink that."

He waves me off with his free hand and pours the lemonade down his throat. Just as quickly as it went down it comes back up. Leon spits it out on the floor of the tent, coughing and gagging. His face turns red and he bends forward, putting his hands on his knees, looking like he's just been punched in the gut.

"What did I tell you."

"Aw. Man. What the hell, where was this shit? Was this shit baking in an oven!"

"What the hell are y'awl doing?" Great we've got the attention of Sgt Evers. "I know you didn't just spit in my tent. Did you just spit all over my tent?"

"Hey Sarge, hey, this shit was burning my throat."

"Well maybe your ass ought not to be taking shit that don't belong to you! I don't recall telling you that you could help yourself to a lemonade."

"Look Sarge, hey we gotta go."

We do? I had no intention of going anywhere.

"Yeah, look, SSgt. Williams needs to see us."

"Y'awl best get moving then."

I shrug my shoulders, with my palms up in the air and whisper to Leon, "Seriously, where are we going?"

"Yeah, we gotta go. Well actually, just you, that's what I came over here for, to tell you SSgt Williams wants to see you in the Scorpion Tent."

"Damn."

Leon slips out of the tent leaving his lemonade bottle spinning circles in the sand on the floor of the tent.

I get up off my cot and I suit up for my walk to SSgt Williams' tent. I start with my desert colored battle dress uniform top, sliding my sweaty arms into the long sleeves and then I button it up. This desert BDU is ridiculous, I look like a big cookie. That's not intimidating. Not at all. How exactly will a big chocolate chip cookie intimidate the enemy? It might make them hungry.

Next is my heavy green camouflage colored flak jacket vest, it's suppose to protect me from shrapnel, slow moving objects, I'm told. As opposed to fast moving objects, like a bullet. This jacket won't stop a bullet and I seriously doubt it will stop any shrapnel either. Let's hope I don't have to find out.

What's next? Most of my stuff is already attached to my vest. My chemical suit is stuffed inside a small waterproof bag that's attached to the back of my vest, it sits between my two, two quart canteens. On the front I have two small ammo pouches, each one has two magazines filled with M16 ammunition. That's about 80 rounds total. Not too bad. There's a loop that's used to hold grenades, but I wasn't issued any grenades. That's just as well, one less thing to carry.

First aid kit, clipped to the front of my vest. Flashlight, also clipped to the front of my vest. Ear plugs, secured in their green plastic container and attached to my vest. Ranger beads, right where they should be, clipped to the front of my vest.

I am not a Ranger, but I've got beads, most soldiers do. The beads are used to help me find my way and keep track of the distance I've traveled if I'm walking somewhere, I don't think I'll be using these beads at all while I'm here.

My bayonet is clipped to my belt, it's kept on my right hip, but I think it should be on my left. It should be on my left because the next thing I'm going to put on is my chemical mask.

My mask.

This thing looks like a Halloween costume. It's a big gray mask with clear bulging eyes, a big black mouth piece and a long gray hood. Right now it's comfortably resting inside its' own private chemical bag. This bag gets strapped around my waist and sits directly over my bayonet. Which is exactly why I think my bayonet should be on my left.

How will I reach my bayonet if I can't get to it because it's sitting underneath my mask? I will not move it to the left though. It will remain where it is since that's what is required. Every soldier in the Army wears their uniform in exactly the same manner, so I can not move it. Everything on every U.S. soldier everywhere in the world is in exactly the same place.

One each, medical cravat, olive drab green in color, that's OD green for short, tied loosely around my neck. I'm not using this cravat for its intended military purpose. Its purpose is to bandage wounds. But I tie it around my neck to keep the dust, dirt, sand and bugs off my neck and to prevent any of that shit from sliding down my shirt. Most of the soldiers here do the same, even though it's not allowed. Look at me, I'm breaking the rules and I'm getting away with it! I feel so liberated.

Camouflage green colored Kevlar helmet, strap that to my head. Goggles, firmly attached to the top of my Kevlar. Finally, the pièce de résistance, my rifle, sling that over my right shoulder, not the left, never the left.

I do one final sweep of equipment, pen, tucked inside my shirt. Notebook, inside my top left pocket, rank, fastened to my collar. Dog tags? One shiny metal tag strung through a chain and hanging around my neck, the other metal tag has been stuffed inside my right boot, just above the tongue of my boot and below the laces. Just in case my upper half gets separated from my lower half, they can identify my remains with my boot tag.

I've got my mismatched hodgepodge uniform and equipment on and I'm ready to walk to the other tent now.

Aw, damn . . . . I gotta take a leak.

Damn it! I'm like a little kid who's been all suited up in a winter snowmobile suit. Forget it, it's gona have to wait, I'm not taking all this shit off just to use the latrine. I'm sweating so much anyway, in a few minutes, I'm not going to have to go anymore anyway.

I head to the Scorpion Tent and I report to SSgt Williams who proceeds to tell me I'm the lucky fucker who has latrine

RICHARD KELLEY

detail today. I knew I couldn't avoid it forever. I'm not sure how I managed to last this long without it. What the hell, I just want to get this shit over with, besides at least I don't have to listen to Evers' mouth anymore, so this isn't going to be all bad is it.

As I leave, I hear Williams' mouth follow me out the door of the Scorpion Tent. "Hey pineapple, don't fuck it up. Don't come crying back here telling me you dicked it up. I don't want to fill out any extra paperwork having to explain why you don't know how to burn shit. You'll be filling out that paper work yourself."

The latrines are, what exactly? Hand-made, home-made outhouses. They're these wood boxes that pretend to be a latrine. There's a wood bench on the inside of the box, with three round holes cut out to form toilets. Underneath the wood holes there are three huge metal containers that collect the waste. Behind the box there are small doors near the metal containers, so you can pull out the containers. Once you pull out the metal containers you need to dispose of the human waste that's been piling up in the containers. There's a whole lot less flies around if you get rid of this shit.

Our method of disposal? Burning. First we line up the metal containers far enough away from the box, so the box doesn't catch on fire. Then we pour gas into the containers. Light a match and toss it into the metal container. Boom. Then we stand around the metal containers and wait for everything to burn away, stirring occasionally, so it all burns through, nothing left behind. Burning all this shit will keep the number of flies lower, at least it should anyway. These flies are relentless.

Back in the States, you can shoo away a fly and he'll leave. But, here? Here, they stay put. Even if you physically swat it away. It'll stay put. When the flies land on your food, you just have to eat around them. They're tough little soldiers. Killing them is the only way to get rid of them. But they've got reinforcements. They'll be back, and they'll come in larger numbers and they'll wear you down.

I know how this enemy works. These flies have been known to collaborate with the scorpions. Fighter-Jet flies,

46

distracting you from above, while the scorpion makes his move on the ground. The flies circle around your head, and the scorpion proceeds with his ground assault. By the time you figure out what's happening, it's too late. You've been ambushed.

I'd like to burn everyone of these flies along with all of the shit I'm burning.

I pull the metal containers out of the latrine and pour gasoline on top of the shit and toilet paper and whatever else has been tossed inside these metal containers.

I pull out my matches, rip out a match and strike it against the back of the matchbook. The match lights up and I toss it into the first container. I repeat the process twice more, one match for each container.

All the containers light up like a couple of backyard grills. Although this doesn't smell anything like a grill.

I can't believe I have to actually stir this shit. I'm stirring shit. Is there a worse job than this? If there is, I don't want to know about it.

"Soldier. Hey soldier."

That must be me that's currently being addressed. I got caught up stirring my shit stew. I turn away from my backyard bar-b-que to see what this asshole has to say to me.

"Soldier! Did you take all three latrine containers out at the same time?"

I size up the dumb-ass captain standing in front of me and I seriously wonder to myself, how did this turd face become a captain when he's too damn stupid to see what's right in front of him. Seriously? I mean, yes, of course I took all three containers out at the same time! He can see it with his own damn captain eyes can't he?

"Yes sir, I did."

"Soldier did it occur to you that someone might need to use the latrine facility during the time you are occupied with your detail? You are to remove the containers one at a time soldier, leaving the rest in place to be used by other individuals."

Other individuals? You don't say? And by other individuals, you must mean other pansy-ass officers like yourself? Dumb-asses who can't take a shit in the sand? Because I'm not a pansy-ass individual, I'm a soldier and I know how to take a shit in the sand without bitching about it.

Forget him. I don't have time to listen to any more garbage this jackass has to say to me, I've got an entire shit bar-b-que going on here. Can't he see I'm busy! I got enough shit to keep me occupied for the entire day.

Is this what they call a shit sandwich? I got shit on both sides of me, I'm sandwiched between the two. Captain Shithead on one side, bar-b-que shit on the other side. Shit!

"Soldier! Are you hearing me soldier?"

Well what the hell does he want me to do about it now? Shall I go get in my time machine your majesty, go back in time and un-take the containers out? Shit! Shit in the sand or wait 'till I'm done fucker! I ignore him, what more can I saw about the topic. I turn back to my shit stew and I stir the pot.

"Soldier. Soldier, this is unacceptable."

Is he still here? He ain't got to shit that bad if he's got all the time in the world to bitch at me. He can go screw himself. But more importantly, he can leave now. I churn my stew and shift my eyes to the side without turning my head so I can see what I can see without actually looking in the direction Captain Shithead. Is he gone yet?

"Soldier!"

"What?" Is all this yelling really necessary? I turn around to see who wants to mess with me now. Aw . . . Hell. It's SSgt. Williams. Daaam. I.T.

"Well holy shit soldier. Holy shit. I heard about it, but I didn't believe it. I just had to see it for myself. You took all those shitting containers out at the same time didn't you soldier? That's absolutely amazing. Now just where in the hell is everybody going to shit while they wait for your ass to finish burning all that shit?"

How the . . . Where? What the? How did he hear about this already? That captain just left. I mean. Captain Shithead literally just left.

"Um. We . . . l.l. they c.a.n."

"What? What did you say soldier? I can't hear you? What did you say?"

I give this some serious thought, thinking it over for a second. I quickly come to the conclusion that it's best not to say a thing to SSgt. Williams, because whatever I do say is going to be the wrong thing to say. I think in a situation like this it's best to just shut up. So I shut up.

"Dam it soldier! You better hope the Colonel doesn't need to use the shitter today. You better hope he ate the cheese and crackers in his MRE and he's backed up."

Ok. Alright then, back to my shit stew.

It feels like 300 degrees standing next to this fire. And this shit stinks, even if it is covered with gasoline, it just smells like . . . Like shit.

What? What was that? A fly? You mother. I shift my head quickly to the left. It's a fly. I hate these flies. Bastards. Where there's one, there's an Army. I know what's next. A scorpion attack. I look down at my feet and shift my eyes from side to side, looking for the unavoidable soon to be approaching scorpion.

Where is he?

I hear another fly buzz around my head and I swat at him with the shovel I'd been using to stir my shit. I miss him but he comes around again. This time I'm ready for the bastard, my shit covered shovel in hand, I crouch down in a wrestler's stance and I eye the sky. Here he comes! I lift my shovel and swing it through the air aiming for the little bastard.

"What the heck, what are you doing! Aaahhh!! Is that poo? Did you just fling poo in my face? What is wrong with you? What are you doing?"

I divert my attention from Operation Fly-Bye and I see Lt. Sheffield. Whoops. There's a splatter of shit across the lieutenant's face. I seriously try my best to hold it in, but I can't. My face starts to crack and I feel a laugh coming out. I quickly turn around and burry my shovel in the shit barrel and start stirring. I can't look at him, I just can't.

I hear Lt. Sheffield storm off bitching as he leaves.

Alright then. Back to my shit. I think in the interest of avoiding any further accidental shit flinging I'm going to put Operation Fly-Bye on hold indefinitely.

I'm busy stirring my shit when I see Leon approaching.

"What is up? Shit detail? That sucks."

"Hey Leon."

"Hey! Hey. Careful with that shovel. I don't want any shit in my face!"

"What? How could you have possibly heard about that already? It just happened!"

"Shit travels fast around here."

"Yeah, right."

"Right in the face? Did you fling shit right in the Lt's face?"

"It was an accident. But yeah, I got him in the face. I mean just a few splatters, you know, not a lot, nothing serious."

"Ha! Ah. Ha. Ha Ha. Ha! That is awesome!"

"Yeah. You think he told SSgt. Williams?"

"Oh hell! SSgt. Williams? Yep, yeah, I'm sure he did."

"Shit."

"Shit. You sure got that right. Ah ha . . . ha. I'm out a here. Keep that shovel in the shit pit."

"Later Leon."

"Later."

I go back to stirring my shit. I notice the sun creeping its way down, headed off to bed. That's good news, heat wise, it's not going to be so hot once the sun sets, but the bad news is, I need to finish burning this shit before the sun sets.

I have three shit filled bar-b-que barrels heavy with the dancing flames of fire. These bright barrels are going to light up the desert. The dancing shit flames on stage for the enemy to see. There are definitely a lot of rules to follow when you're in the Army and even more when you're in a combat zone. Light and noise discipline is one of the many rules here that is actually followed.

Discipline. The use of the word makes it seem like you need to scold the light and noise for being too bright and loud. It's really much simpler than that, light and noise discipline means don't make any noise and don't use any lights.

Well, I mean you can use lights, you just can't use lights at night. You can use them during daylight hours, when the enemy won't notice you're using lights. So during the day, you turn the lights on, and at night you turn the lights off.

Simple Army logic.

Those rules apply to all lights, everywhere. The lights in your tent, the headlights on your vehicle, you have to turn those off at night and then turn them on during the day. Don't even think about using a flashlight at night, but you better make sure you always have it with you, it's part of your uniform.

That discipline rule applies to noise too, you're not allowed make any noise either. Using lights at night and making loud noises will give away your position to the enemy. So these three shit barrels of flames will alert the enemy to our location. I definitely have to hurry up and finish burning this shit.

So I hurry up.

I'm not too convinced that light and noise discipline really makes much of a difference because this rifle of mine is pretty damn loud when I fire it and when you're in the desert you can see everything for miles and miles. There isn't any real camouflage in the desert but it's a theory I'm not willing to test out at the moment, so I'm going to close the shit kitchen just as soon as I can.

I put the metal containers back into the latrine and close the small door at the back of the wood box. I think those containers are still pretty hot since they've been on fire all morning and most of the afternoon, but no one's going to sit their ass directly on the metal containers anyway. There's wood toilet seats over the top of the metal containers, so it should be fine. But that's another theory I don't want to test out, so I'm going to get out of here before someone comes around to use the shitter and bitch about their hot ass.

After an afternoon of burning shit, I'm covered in black soot and outhouse fragrance. I smell like shit and I look like it too. I head off to take a shower.

With the sun finally setting, it's no longer as hot as it had been throughout the day. Right now it's just warm, but when the sun sets it gets real cold real fast. The sand can't soak up the sun and maintain its heat the way a dirt and grass covered ground can.

The noise discipline rule seems to be working, because it's quiet here, real quiet and real dark. I look up towards the dark sky and see a sea of stars. I never realized there were so many stars, it's so dark here it's easy to see every star, no bright lights around to dull the view of the sky. I've never seen anything like this before, star after star they're all bold and bright. Since I'm not able to use my flashlight to light my way, I'm glad to have a bight sky filled with stars and a full moon above me lighting up my path to the shower.

There are so few moments like this in the desert, moments that are pleasant and free from battle, free from bombs and enemies, free from officers and stupid details, free from responsibility. I like it. It's peaceful.

I hear a loud slam. I recognize it instantly as wood on wood. It's the shower door slamming shut. I wonder if that's someone leaving the shower or if it's someone entering it. There aren't any secrets in that big box. You can't be shy either, not if you want to take a shower. You just have to get in and get out, ignore your naked neighbor, get yourself clean and then get out of there. It's mostly men here in our unit, but there's a light sprinkling of females here and we all use the same shower. So, one more reason to get in and get out, so to speak, as quickly as possible.

"Hey."

"Hey." Sgt. Destino? Well now! I should have been at this shower sooner. No, that's wrong. We're both soldiers and I shouldn't be thinking about another soldier like that.

"It's getting late. Where you coming from?"

"Shit burning detail." That was stupid! Why did I say that? That's what I want, Sgt Destino having an image of me burning shit. Well, forget about it, I know I smell like shit, at least it will be clear that I don't usually smell like this and the only reason I smell like shit is because I've been burning it all day.

"So that was you that hit Lt. Sheffield in the face with shit?"

"It was an accident." Even through the darkness I see Sgt. Destino smile, not laugh, but just smile. It's a nice smile and smiles are in short supply in this miserable place. It makes me smile. Then I look at the rest of Sgt. Destino who's wearing nothing but a towel and isn't shy about it. There's no rush to cover up or find another towel or put clothes on. Such boldness. I like it.

This is wrong. We're both soldiers. This is a fellow soldier I'm thinking about like this. But damn. Still wet too.

"Alright, I gotta go, you have a good night."

"Good night Sergeant."

I turn around to watch the sergeant walk away, lucky for me the stars are lighting up the area pretty good, so I can see plenty. Plenty.

I really stink, I think that might explain the sergeant's rush to get out of here. I take off my uniform and consider tossing it in the trash, it's probably going to smell like shit forever.

The big wood box showers look a lot like the latrine, except that these wood boxes have a metal container on the top that's attached to a heater to warm up the water. There's a handle on the inside of the shower, I pull it and release the water from inside the heated metal container. I savor the brief moment before the water hits me, knowing that after spending a shit filled day it's going to end with the luxury of a hot shower. Here comes the water!

Fuck! The water is cold. No, not cold, it's freezing, it feels like I'm standing inside a freezer and I'm getting a glass of ice water dumped on my head. Now that the sun has set it's also cold outside, and there's a breeze, I never expected a shower to be torture, but it is.

I try to soap up and rinse off as quick as I can. I had been looking forward to this moment all day and now I just want to get out of this shower and end the torture as soon as possible.

I hear the shower door open and slam shut again, wood hitting wood. I wonder with a brief moment of enthusiasm if Sgt. Destino has returned. Maybe I'm not in such a hurry to get out this shower after all.

I look to the door and immediately realize my mistake, I should not have looked. It's the First Sergeant who walked in and without warning has striped down to his bare ass.

This is where I should make some unflattering comments about having to look at a naked First Sergeant, but what possible words could describe a sight like that?

SIX

BANANAS

My CD player is broken, what a catastrophe. At first I thought it was the batteries that were the problem, but I just put brand new batteries in it and it still doesn't work. I have a radio, but that's not really the same as being able to listen to your favorite song when you really want to hear it.

Besides the only station that comes in on this radio is the BBC. All the British ever do is talk . . . talk . . . talk. Talk . . . . They never play any music, and that's really all I want. I want to hear music. I want to listen to my favorite songs, I want to hear my music.

I hadn't anticipated that not having music would bother me so much. There are a lot of things that go on here in the desert that could be described as torture, but not having music has got to be the absolute worst. I try to remember the words to songs, any songs. I start to replay them in my head.

It's hard to recall all the exact words to songs. How many times in my life have I listened to one particular song and sang along with it word for word and now I can't remember the words. I close my eyes and stop thinking so hard about it, I try to let the words just come to me, hoping I remember.

I leave my headphones on even though there's no sound coming from them, they help drown out the noise in my tent. The headphones also form a physical stop sign that keeps some people from bothering me. If anyone sees me wearing them most people won't bother talking to me. Most people anyway and being left alone around here is usually a pretty good thing. Because just about every time someone here has something to say it's something I would rather not hear.

I'm lying on my cot sweating as usual, going over the words in my head of the songs I can remember when Staff Sergeant Williams busts into our tent and starts yelling at all of us. "Hey turds! Clean up this filthy banana garden! It's a shit pit in here!"

I look around at our tent. It is disgusting in here. Everyone always leaves their stuff laying all over the place. I'm not sure where all this stuff comes from, it's a mystery to me. Maybe all this stuff was sent to them from home. I know they didn't arrive here with all this stuff and the only place around here you can go to buy anything new is the Post Exchange and there's only one around here that I know of and it's about an hour from where we are right now.

I don't know why anyone would bother to buy anything at the PX here anyway. Whatever you buy is going to get ruined by all the sand and then what are you going to do with it when it's time to leave and go back home? We all arrived here with two duffle bags and one ruck sack and we're all going to be leaving with the same two duffle bags and ruck sack that we came with. There won't be any room in our bags to put the stuff so it will have to be thrown out and left behind. That seems like a waste to me and all that stuff is taking up space in a tent that's already too crowded.

SSgt. Williams continues on with the daily rant, "Well holy garden gnomes, I didn't know I was living next door to a tent full of farm animals. Did you pigs forget to put your request in for maid service this morning?" SSgt. Williams walks through the tent, eyeing each cot and kicking shit out of the way. "This damn bus terminal better be shit-free by the time I get back here, and you can believe I'm coming back."

One Private inadvertently gets a little too close to Sergeant Williams, "Well holy shit sandwich Private, what the hell are you doing just standing around? Are you too good to clean up your barnyard?" The Private doesn't say a word, opting to just stare at SSgt. Williams instead. I'm not sure that's the choice I would've made.

"Private. Where are your pants? Are you actually standing here talking to me without any pants on? Is this even your tent soldier? Never mind. Never mind, it doesn't matter. Just clean it up!"

Staff Sergeant Williams lets out a long whistle, "You hear that Private?" SSgt. Williams cups a hand around an ear in a mock attempt to listen. "Listen. That's the train to clean-it-up town . . . . You better get on board Private!!"

Williams throws a fist in the air and pulls down and back up again, repeating the motion and making the train whistle sound again while continuing the march down the center of the tent and heads out the door at the opposite end of the tent. "I'll be back turds."

I usually dread listening to the daily commands being spit out of SSgt. Williams mouth, but this one isn't so bad because this tent is a mess and if the soldiers in this tent aren't told to clean it up they're not going to clean it up.

I get stuck with garbage detail in this clean-up catastrophe. I think garbage detail is going to be a lot less miserable than the shit burning detail I had. I hope it's a long time before I get that detail again. Picking up garbage might suck, but it's going to be better than lying on my cot sweating. I can walk around and sweat now

I take my time and I suit up with all my required military gear and equipment. I put on one piece of equipment at a time, everything is always in the same place. I carry everything with me everywhere I go nothing is left behind. I head outside the tent and step into the bright afternoon sun.

So I'm supposed to collect all the garbage from the area and get rid of it. Get rid of it where? Where am I supposed to take it? This isn't like shit-burning detail. I know what to do with that. I don't know what to with the garbage.

Fortunately or unfortunately, I'm not sure yet, I've got Sergeant Valetta working with me. He should know what to do with this garbage right? He's a noncommissioned officer after all and NCO's know how to get shit done. Maybe not. He seemed just as baffled as I am.

We start at my tent first and pick up all the garbage bags that have accumulating and then we move on to Sgt. Valetta's tent. We roam through the heat and the sand collecting all the garbage bags from the area, picking them up one at a time.

I wonder what everyone else did with the trash bags when they had garbage detail. Where would they have taken it? Maybe I should've asked someone who's had this detail before. No, forget that, that would just make me look stupid. I'll figure it out. I mean really, it's just trash, how difficult could it be to get rid of it.

As we walk through the area I notice everybody in the unit is cleaning something. I guess SSgt. Williams paraded through everyone's tent and got on them about cleaning up. Walking around and picking up bags is probably one of the easier jobs around here.

It takes us most of the afternoon to collect all the trash. It takes us so long, not necessarily because there are so many bags, but because it's so hot and neither one of us has the energy to move very fast in this heat. The heat drains the life out of a soldier and slows us down.

It's hard to move fast when you're hot and sweaty and weighted down with all this military equipment and it's even harder to move fast when your life isn't at stake and you're doing something you would rather not be doing. Picking up trash isn't something I want to be doing.

All this military gear I am wearing slows down the process even more. But we're not allowed to take any of it off when we're outside the tent. Inside the tent is a different story, inside the tent we could be naked if we really wanted. I don't want to be. But outside the tent we have to wear each and every piece of our military equipment and wear it in the exact spot it belongs.

Once we have all the garbage bags gathered up, neither one of us is sure what we're suppose to do with them.

I ask Sgt Valetta how we're supposed to carry all this garbage. He looks intently at the bags and then looks around our site as if the solution lies somewhere out in the desert. He decides we need a vehicle. Neither one of us is important enough to have been issued our own vehicle so we start walking around the area looking for a vehicle that's not locked.

We notice Colonel Bahanda's humvee isn't locked and we decide to take it. Colonel Bananas isn't going to miss his vehicle, he's not even around and his driver is a dumb-ass for leaving the shit unsecured. Besides we're just going to use it to dump this garbage and then we're going to return it.

We load up the back of the Colonel's truck with all the garbage. It's overflowing with plastic garbage bags. I ask him where we're taking it and Sgt. Valetta says we're just going to drive this shit out into the desert far enough away from the area and dump it, maybe burry it. His guess is as good as mine.

He tells me to just drive and we'll figure it out when we get somewhere. It's dark now so I'm not able to use the lights. Light and noise discipline is always in effect. I guess that's good, not using the lights because then no one will see us using Colonel Banana's vehicle. But I can't really see where I'm going without any lights. I should be used to driving in the dark by now, but I'm not.

I turn the ignition switch and I wait for the wait light to go out before I can start up the engine. Supposedly the glow plugs are warming up, getting hot enough to start the engine, kind of like spark plugs. But the diesel fuel in this engine won't spark up like gasoline does. I didn't believe it at first, but I've actually seen someone put a cigarette out in a puddle of diesel fuel.

Wait. Wait for the wait light. Even the Army vehicles have me waiting. Only in the Army could there be an actual light that lights up on the dashboard telling a soldier to wait, the bright yellow light actually has the word WAIT written on it. Wait. Alright I get it. I do a lot of waiting in the Army. Can I go now?

Finally! The wait light goes out on the dashboard and I start the engine and we take off.

I'm driving away with the Colonel's truck loaded up with plastic garbage bags and I begin to feel a little bad. I think about what's going to happen if we get caught basically stealing the Colonel's hummer. Not only are Sgt. Valetta and I going to get in trouble, but the Colonel's driver is going to be in deep shit too, since he's the one who left the vehicle unlocked.

But now that I'm actually doing it, I don't really care who gets caught, or who gets in trouble. I feel a little rush of excitement. I'm glad that it's dark and Sgt Valetta can't see this stupid grin on my face.

I feel a little sense of freedom as I'm driving through the dark desert. No lights, no permission, no destination, no rules, I didn't even bother to put my seat belt on.

I open up my window and I let the warm breeze flow in and hit me in the face. I look out through the front windshield and I see the sky filled stars, it's hard to comprehend there are so many.

I start to speed up a little. This is great! We fly through the desert ignoring all the rules.

Bang!

Oh shit! What was that? After I hear the loud thunk noise, the hummer stops moving. Oh shit. I look at the Sergeant and he looks at me. I put the parking brake on, although I'm not sure the vehicle really needs it at this point and we get out of the vehicle and check out the scene. It's really dark, so it's hard to see what's going on. But we find a small 1.5 kilowatt generator wedged underneath the truck.

Sgt. Valetta tells me to get back in and just keep going. He says if I was able to drive over it, I should be able to drive off of it. Sounds good to me. But he's wrong. I put the humvee in drive and I try to pull forward, I put it in reverse and I try to back off the generator, but it doesn't work. The more I spin my tires the deeper they dig themselves into the sand and further onto the generator. No matter how hard we try, this thing is stuck. It's wedged on top of the generator. It's not going anywhere. But we are.

We decide to leave it just as it is. Colonel Banana's vehicle is all loaded up with garbage bags, wedged on top of a generator and unsecured. Damn, the Colonel's driver is going to be in deep shit. The hell with it. We get out of the vehicle and leave. I'm not worried about it, really, because I know karma will get even with me later, or sooner.

I go back to my tent so I can lie on my cot to sweat and wait to get bit during the night by all the various vampire insects that come out at night to suck my blood. I can go to sleep completely dressed from head to toe and I will still wake up in the morning with fresh bites. They can chew through clothes or crawl under them or something, I'm not sure.

What I am sure of is there's not a spot left on my body that hasn't been bitten yet. I'm covered with insect welts, tiny red ones, big swollen lumps and mid-size welts, you name it, I've got it. Every single bite itches like poison ivy, so on top of all the bug welts I've got scratch marks across my skin as well from all the itching and scratching I do. At least my entire body stays covered up with my uniform so no one has to see all the welts and scratches because it's starting to look pretty bad.

I use insect repellent, I pour it on like I'm taking a shower in it but it doesn't do any good. I think these bugs like the smell of insect repellent. I've even use flea collars, the ones that are usually hanging around the neck of a cat or dog. I have one on each wrist tucked under my BDU sleeve and one wrapped around each ankle, just above my boot and underneath my pant leg. I keep them hidden underneath my uniform, because if they are seen by anyone then I would be considered out of uniform and I would have to take them off. Every Army uniform must look exactly like every other Army uniform in the world and flea collars are not part of the uniform.

The insects aren't as bad during the day, with the exception of the flies, during the day the flies are insane. They're everywhere and they go anywhere they want, they do not move even if you swat at them, they stay put. They walk across your food leaving a trail of fly-prints across your breakfast like they own the place. It's impossible to eat anything without having a few flies walk across it first. That can't be good for my stomach because I know that before those flies walked on my food they were walking on shit in the latrine.

I've really got to get a mosquito net. I wonder if they have any extra nets in supply. I take a detour from heading to my tent and I go to the supply tent. I hope like all get out they have an extra net because I don't think I can take another night of being dinner to the vampire insects. I don't think there is a spot left on my body that hasn't been attacked by those dirty little blood sucking vampire insects.

Crap!

How in the hell did I not remember that Sergeant Pancakes was the supply sergeant. Well . . . I'm never actually at supply and Sgt. Pancakes is someone I'd like to forget about anyway, so I can see how I didn't remember.

"Howdy do soldier."

"Hey sergeant."

"What the hoodle brings you to my supply tent?"

Hoodle? I feel myself getting a headache. "Yeah. I just wanted to know if you had a mosquito net?"

Sergeant Pancakes leans forward into me practically singing out his response to me. "A mosquito net . . . ???"

I don't really get the game he's playing and I'm actually kind of tired. Is this karma getting even with me already? I let out a long sigh and I toss up my hands, "I don't know Sergeant, just a mosquito net. Do you have one?"

"Do you have one . . . ???" He puts his hands on his hips and smiles, apparently waiting for my response in this chorus line jingle game.

"What? What Sergeant, what are you getting at?"

"Begins with a P . . ." He leans in towards me again with a look of expectant hopefulness.

Begins with a P? Please. You have got to be kidding me. "Sergeant may I have a mosquito net please?"

"There you go soldier!" His face lights up with a smile. "Please will get you plenty."

"Alright then. So how about that net then, so I can get off to bed?"

Sergeant Pancakes clasps his hands together, makes a sad face and tilts his head to one side, "Yeah, sorry soldier, but I'm fresh out of nets."

I let out another long sigh, this is bananas. It's late, I'm tired, it's been a long day and I have a headache. Why he bothered with that big production number knowing full well he didn't even have any nets I'll never know. "Alright, well thanks anyway Sergeant." I leave the supply sergeant and walk back to my tent.

It's really dark. There's just a piece of the moon showing and a bunch of stars illuminating the sky. I snap my flashlight off its clip and flip the switch to turn it on. It's got a red lens covering the light beam so it doesn't light up very much. I'm told the red lens prevents the enemy from using infrared detection to locate our position when we use lights at night.

Does that really work? I haven't a clue. I'm not sure what the point is considering we're in the middle of the desert and you can see everything for miles around anyway.

And at this particular point all of that is irrelevant. Why? Because the batteries in my flashlight are through. I could have sworn I just changed the batteries in my flashlight. I shake it and smack it against my hand in the hopes that might actually do something to change the situation, but of course it does nothing to rectify the situation.

"Need a light?"

I'm not going to admit that the voice from out of know where in the dark scared me even if it looks like I may have jumped out of my boots. Because I'm a soldier and soldiers don't get scared, not even when someone approaches them in the dark in the middle of a combat zone.

It's really dark, but even so I can see enough detail to identify my night time oogiety boogiety.

Sergeant Destino.

Alright now. This day is shaping up after all.

SEVEN

DIRECTIONS

We are going to another new location today. We spent the morning tearing down our site, packing up all the equipment on the vehicles and filling in all of the foxholes. We will be leaving the area so it looks like we were never here at all. A silent, faceless, nameless soldier came here, did their job and left without a trace. That's how it's done. That's how it will be done when I return to the United States, I will leave no evidence for anyone to let them know I was ever a soldier, I will leave no evidence that I was ever here. That's how a soldier moves through the world.

Faceless. Nameless.

We spend a lot of time waiting. I've been awake since five o'clock this morning. That's the usual time we get up around here. Some days I don't see the point to getting up so early in the morning because we spend most of the day waiting. I think all that time could have been better spent sleeping in.

Everything in our unit has been torn down, packed up, filled in or thrown out so all that's left to do is wait. Wait to be told it's time to start our vehicles and move to another location. Each time we move, we move closer to the Iraqi border. Things have been happening fast so we've been moving a lot. It's easy to tell we've been moving closer to the border because the sounds of the bombs from the air war have been getting louder.

I climb into the passenger's seat of the vehicle I'll be riding in during this move. I don't have my own vehicle, so I switch around a lot to different vehicles every time we move. Occasionally I drive, but usually I'm just a passenger along for the ride. Either way, it doesn't really matter to me as long as I get put in a vehicle with someone decent, I don't mind.

The convoy commander makes out the list and decides who will be in what vehicle and who will drive and what order the vehicles will be in for the convoy. I get no say in the matter.

"Afternoon soldier."

"Hey, Chief Morgan, what's up?"

"It looks like we are going to be keeping each other company during this drive."

"Is that right? Alright now."

"You need anything before we take off?"

"Naw, Chief, I'm ready to go. The vehicle's ready to go too, I took care of it, we're all set"

"We're just waiting on the word then?"

"Looks like it."

"Alright then, wake me up when it's time to go."

"Not a problem Chief."

Chief Morgan is a cool shit. There are not too many people around like him. Look at him, just like that, he falls asleep on the hood of the truck. So, calm, not a worry in the world. Well, what do I really know? Just because something looks a certain way doesn't make it true. Maybe he's all kinds of worried about stuff, who knows? But he sure knows how to not let it show if he is worried about anything.

He's really intelligent though, maybe that's the secret ingredient to taking things in stride, being smart enough to know how to deal with stress.

"What is up?"

"Hey Leon, what's up with you?"

"Not a thing. Just waiting on the word to go."

"Yeah. I'm not in any hurry to go, because as soon as we get there, we're going to have to set all this equipment up again."

"Eh." Leon waves a hand in the air, brushing off the upcoming work. He doesn't say much, but I get the point, why worry about what may or may not happen in the future. There's no guarantee we'll actually arrive at our destination. More importantly, even if we do arrive and we have to set everything up, why worry about that now. We should just live in the moment we have now. A moment without any work.

Leon takes out his pack of cigarettes and shakes one out of the pack. He offers me one and I take it. He lets the cigarette dangle off the edge of his lips while he fishes through his BDU's searching for a lighter. He pats his front shirt pockets, shoves his hands in his front pants pockets, taps his back pockets, slides his hands down the sides of his cargo pockets and back up again to pat his top pockets one more time.

"Hell."

"Ammo pouch."

"What? What the shit did I do with my lighter?"

"It's inside your ammo pouch." His face lights up like an illuminating light bulb.

"That's right."

He unhooks the clasp on the green ammo pouch that's hooked to the front of his belt. He digs his fingers inside the pouch and pulls out his lighter, like a magician pulling a rabbit out of a hat and holds it up to the sky.

"Ta-da!"

He lights his cigarette and then hands his lighter over to me so I can light mine. "Thanks Leon."

"He inhales and blows the smoke out. "Hey not a problem."

He keeps smoking and nods towards the front of the vehicle. "You riding with Chief Morgan?"

"What's the matter, you jealous?'

"Naw, hell no. You want to trade?"

"No. Hell no. Who you riding with?"

"Sergeant Destino."

"Bullshit."

Leon leans on the open door of the vehicle, sticking half his body through the window and inhales more smoke and lets out a short laugh that lets me know he's full of it. "That'd be sweet wouldn't it?"

I nod and smile. Instantly my mind starts to wander to last night when I was walking back to my tent and ran into Sgt. Destino. I think about the growing interest between us. We spend a lot of time talking to each other, getting closer to each other, not physically close, but just getting to know each other better.

It's nice to have someone that makes my day less shitty. Someone I look forward to seeing, someone I like talking to. Someone who's starting to make me think about . . . .

"Start 'em up, let's go!"

The convoy commander, Colonel Bahanda stands at the front of the convoy and whistles. "Let's go, let's go!"

"Hey I'll talk to you later Leon."

"Alright, later."

I step out of the vehicle and tap on the hood. "Hey Chief. Chief!"

Chief Morgan stirs and turns his head to face me, "What's going on?"

"Time to go Chief."

"Alright now."

Chief slides off the hood of the truck and climbs into the driver's seat, wait's for the wait light and then starts up the vehicle. We wait for the vehicle in front of us to move and then we take off, following along in the convoy.

We keep a far distance between ourselves and the vehicle in front of us. That distance is to ensure our safety, because if we get hit with any sort of bombs or rifle fire, we will be spread out far enough that it will be unlikely every vehicle in the convoy or the soldiers in it will be destroyed or killed all at the same time.

This method of being spread out will ensure there will be some of us left alive to keep moving forward to our destination so we can continue fighting this war.

That's also the reason why the convoy commander takes such a long time making out the list of drivers and passengers and puts such effort into deciding the order of the vehicles. It's important not to put two similar vehicles right next to each other, they have to be separated so they don't both get taken out at the same time.

The maintenance vehicle always goes last in the event a vehicle breaks down they'll stop with the truck and fix it while the remainder of the convoy keeps traveling along, following the convoy commander who always goes first, leading the way to our destination.

It must be quite a sight to see a military convoy ride past. The long line of tan colored vehicles, their loud engines shaking the ground, the tires kicking up sand as we roll by. The wind blowing over our trail of tire tracks behind us, covering up our presence. We blow in with a fuss and loud noises and then we disappear into the desert like we were never even here.

We drive through the desert surrounded by the view of sand all around us. The sun is hot and the air is dry. It feels heavy in my lungs to breathe in the hot, dry air. It's impossible to breathe in without feeling like you're also gulping sand into your lungs with each breath.

Sometimes it's actually painful to breathe.

This particular drive is supposed to take six hours, but we had only been driving for about an hour and a half when the convoy commander makes an unscheduled stop. An unscheduled stop is never good.

Do I even want to know what's going on? It wouldn't matter if I did want to know what's going on, because low life pieces of shit privates like me never get any information. We just get told what to do.

I ask my driver, Chief Morgan why nobody ever tells us what's going on. Is it really that hard to pass along information.

Morgan lets out a small chuckle, "You want to know why nobody ever tells you anything soldier? It's simple. You simply aren't anyone of importance. You are a soldier, and you are nothing but a soldier. That's why nobody tells you anything, you aren't worthy of knowing soldier. You're not even worthy of an identity, why do you think we all dress alike and look alike?"

"I'm more than that Chief, that's not all I'll ever be. I am a soldier right now, but that's not who I'll always be."

"That isn't who you are soldier, that's what you are. All of us, we aren't anything more than property, government property. Property of the United States government."

"Property? Well I'm not going to be property forever Chief, I'm not going to be in the Army forever. I'm getting out of the Army as soon as I leave here."

"You might get out of the desert, you might even get out of the Army soldier, but the Army has no intention of getting out of you. All this mess here, you might think you're going to leave it behind, but you aren't. You can't. You're a soldier for life."

Chief Morgan gets out of the vehicle and walks towards the front of the convoy. I think about the Chief's words of wisdom and I wonder how right he is about the Army never leaving me. Will I carry this experience with me for the rest of my life wherever I go? Will it always be on my mind, will it live under the surface or will it blatantly display itself on the surface? Will these waking hour nightmares return to me in my sleep year after year?

How will I get the Army out of me and move on with my life? Will the Army leave me without leaving a trace of its presence behind? According to the Chief that's not the way the Army moves through a soldier, it stays with them for life. I had not anticipated that.

The Chief comes back to our vehicle and informs me of the reason for the convoy's unscheduled stop. Colonel Bahanda is lost and he's asking some Iraqis for directions.

Are you serious? Who asks the enemy for directions? Alright, well while the leader of this unit is busy asking the enemy for directions I'm going to make good use of my time.

I have got to take a leak and the use of a restroom is a luxury I don't have anymore. I look around for a place to go. I could just go right out here in the open with the entire unit in sight, but I don't want to. We're surrounded by several large sand hills. I decide to use one of them as my own personal latrine. I walk towards the sand hill and I get stopped and warned not to leave the road we were traveling on because there are several landmines and Iraqi booby-traps off the road.

I know I'm being a little ridiculous with my desire for privacy but I don't care. I have to go, I can't hold it any longer and I want some privacy. I venture out beyond the sand hill and I turn it into my own personal latrine.

I feel so much better. Not just because I was able to relieve myself, but it's the privacy that gives me a brief moment of feeling human again. Everything is so in the open here, every last private detail of your life is shared with the rest of the unit every single day. It feels good to have a moment alone for such a personal act. How many times had I taken privacy for granted when I used the bathroom back in the states?

The Chief's words return to my head again and I wonder if the simple act of going to the bathroom will be tarnished forever after being here. Will I be able to walk into a bathroom and take it for granted or will I have this place and this experience lingering in the back of my mind every time I walk into a bathroom?

These thoughts feel too heavy on my mind and I don't want to think about them. It's better to just be in the moment anyway. Who knows how long any of us have anyway. Maybe I won't even live long enough to get out of this desert and I won't have to worry about memories about this place. Hmmm . . . Well. That thought is even heavier than the first thought I was trying to get out of my mind. This place can really wreck havoc on a person's mind.

Let me just move forward, keep walking, that's all I can do at the moment. Maybe if I keep myself moving I won't spend as much time thinking. That's the real torture of this place, all the time I have to think. All this time to think about things, is a little overwhelming.

As I'm returning to my vehicle I feel something tugging on my foot and I immediately stop in my tracks and I look down. I see nothing unusual. I keep looking at my feet and I pick them up one at a time. Once again I feel something pulling on my foot.

Shit . . . .

I call for Sgt. Evers, who happens to be the closet person to me. I'm silently wishing someone else had been closer to me, someone other than Sergeant fat-ass. But at the moment she's all I've got. She looks irritated and takes her time walking over to me.

I explain the situation to her. She doesn't see anything either. She tells me not to move, and then she leaves to get help.

I try not to let my mind believe I'm going to die, but it's useless. Although Sgt. Evers seemed calm I could sense the fear in her eyes. Without speaking a word I knew we both believed I had stumbled across a booby-trap.

I get angry with myself for ignoring the previous warning I received about not leaving the road. How could I have been so stupid? Did I really want privacy so much that I am willing to risk my life for it? Why were my latrine adventures always getting me into trouble?

I stand perfectly still for what feels like an eternity, but it was only a few seconds. Sgt. Evers quickly returns with several others. Surprisingly fast they find what had been tugging at my foot.

A wire.

A wire thinner than a strand of hair that had been used for an expelled wire-guided missile. Remnants of what remained of the missile. I was safe. Have I learned my lesson? Will I continue to search for privacy and the brief feeling of humanity that comes along with it even if it means risking my life? I don't know.

I walk back to the truck Chief Morgan and I have been riding in. He's lying on the hood of the vehicle and he's got his BDU hat covering his face. The Chief is always so relaxed, not a care in the world. I could take a lesson from the Chief because I think sometimes I'm wound a little too tight. I've got to relax.

I don't know how he does it. He seems like he's made peace with the world around him. It's like he's somehow seen the future and he's ok with it. Well he is older, maybe that's the secret. Age. Wisdom. But he's not that old. 53 isn't exactly old. It's Army old that's for sure. But it's not old. Maybe he's been through so much in his life, it just gets easier to take things in stride because you know you're going to make it through to the other side and still be alright.

After 53 years of life's experiences I would think you should be content with a lot of things. I would think a person would have learned a lot of lessons by then and they truly know what's important in the world and what's worth being upset over and what's just a waste of time worrying about.

Maybe he's just drunk.

He does always have a drink in his hand and I know it looks like iced tea, but maybe it's whiskey. I know a shot of whiskey sure would make me pretty content right about now.

"Hey soldier, where did you get off too?"

"Hey Chief. I just went to use the latrine." No point in telling him about my almost-near-death experience. Not because it will worry him, because I don't think much of anything worries the Chief, but I don't want to tell him because I don't want a lecture right now.

I feel bad enough already. I know the Chief wouldn't intentionally try to make me feel bad, but his words have a way of sticking to me. I already feel stupid enough for getting caught up in a wire-guided missile wire and needing Sgt. Evers help after being warned about walking off the road.

I also feel like I might disappoint Chief Morgan if I tell him about what happened. I'm not sure where this feeling is coming from. I have never once in my life worried about disappointing someone. Honestly, I've never had anyone to disappoint. This is new to me and I'm not sure what this means or what I'm supposed to do now.

Maybe it will all work itself out. I don't know. But what I do know is that being around the Chief has changed me, his insightfulness, his laid back way of approaching the world, his intelligence. He gives me direction in my life. Something I've never had before. I feel like things are going to be different in my life. I feel like I can accomplish things in my life that I never thought I could before. I feel like I can make something out of my life when I get out of here. I feel different. I think that's because I'm doing something I've never done before, and that something is feeling.

I feel.

I'm not sure what to do with this information and this new ability to feel and my new found ability to give a shit about another human being and my ability to worry about what someone else thinks about me.

We get the signal to start our vehicles and get ready to move out. That's good because movement clears my mind of all the thoughts I seem to constantly have in my head. Sitting still gives me too much time to think.

Another long and boring drive through the desert. The hardest part about these long boring drives is staying awake. The heat is really intense and makes me sleepy, then there's the heat from the engine that intensifies the heat even more. The sound of the engine is a loud steady hum that has this weird relaxing quality to it that lulls me to sleep.

Then of course there's just nothing at all to look at. Sun and sand and that's it. Fortunately I'm not driving during this move. It always seems harder to stay awake when you're driving.

It helps to have someone decent like Chief Morgan to talk to during the drive, but the engine is so loud you literally have to yell over the sound of the engine to be heard. That's a plus when you're riding with someone you'd rather not talk to because you can let the sound of the engine drown out their words.

We arrive at out new destination and the first thing we have to do is set up the Colonel's tent. The process is always the same at each new location. The sleeping tents are always set up first, starting with the tent of the highest ranking person until finally we set up the tent with the lowest ranking soldiers, that would be my tent.

After all the sleeping tents are set up, then we set up the generators, so there's power in all the tents, that's mostly just for lights. In our tent, that equals two single dangling light bulbs, that barely illuminate the tent at night. We're allowed to use the lights inside our tent as long as all the tent openings are closed so no one can see the lights from outside the tent.

It usually takes a few hours to set up all the tents and generators, so it's usually pretty late by the time we get all of that finished and then we just go to sleep so we can get up early the next morning and continue with the set up.

The rest of the set up involves, putting together the shower and latrine, digging foxholes, unloading equipment and personal items from the vehicles, setting up the mess tent for dinning and putting up radar scattering camouflage netting over the tents.

That whole process takes about three days to accomplish and about three hours to tear it all down when we move to a new location.

The benefit to having all this work to do is that it keeps my mind occupied as well. Boredom is really hard to overcome, because with boredom comes thinking. I don't like having all that time to think about things. Thinking about my current situation isn't time well spent.

My body takes a beating when we set up the unit. It gets banged around a lot, I get hit with tent poles, camouflage nets fall on my head, hammers drop on my feet, I get whacked in the arm with metal tent pegs and duffle bags bounce off my legs.

My body is quite a sight at this moment. I have bruises everywhere from all the banging around, swollen itchy insect bites that I scratch until they bleed, sunburn across any exposed skin, sand ground into my hair and red, raw blisters covering my feet. I've lost a few pounds and I didn't have many pounds to spare to begin with. I sweat constantly and I only get to shower a few times a week. I wash my uniforms by hand in a dirty, plastic yellow tub and then I hang them up in my stale tent to dry and then put them back on again.

I wake up earlier than usual the next morning. It's only four in the morning and I can't get back to sleep. I decide to put on my physical training uniform and go for a run. This early in the morning it will be cool enough to run.

I can't go very far away from our unit because it would be too dangerous, so I just run circles around our perimeter. It's hard to run in the sand. My foot sinks in each time I hit the ground and I have to pull my feet out every time they hit the sand.

Usually my PT uniform consists of gray shorts and a t-shirt, but because I'm in a combat zone, I have to keep my protective mask with me. It's strapped to my side and it bounces up and down with every stride. I keep my rife with me at all times, even now while I'm running. I use the strap to sling it across my back. The rifle strap is a little tighter than the one on my mask so it stays put better and doesn't bounce around as much while I'm running. The dog tag hanging around my neck makes a quiet racket as it tinks against the metal chain.

So much for noise discipline. All this equipment jingle jangling around seems rather loud to me. As long as no one's complaining I'm going to keep on running.

I time myself and I run circles for twenty minutes. I have no clue how many miles that adds up to, probably not as many as I could usually run. I don't think the mask and the rife slowed me down much, but I think the sand really slowed me down. Every step I take sinks into the sand and it takes a lot of effort to pull my feet out of the sand and take my next step. I'm sweating more than usual after I run and I probably didn't run nearly as far as it felt.

As soon as I finish running I realize my mistake. We just moved to our new location and we haven't had time to set up the showers yet.

Damn.

I'm not going to be able to take a shower and I'm going to stink more than usual today. That's good. Maybe people will leave me alone today then. Besides I keep hearing that the more you stink the less the bugs will bother you. Apparently they don't like stinky people. Well, alright. I'm pretty stinky and there's not much I can do about it right now, so let's just see how much the insects are going to bother me.

So, alright then, people don't like the stink and bugs don't like the stink. I might just have a pretty good day today without anyone or anything bothering me.

If this works I just might run every morning.

EIGHT

PB & Js

Staff Sergeant Williams sends Specialist Leon and me on a mission to pick up food rations for the Iraqi enemy prisoners of war. I'm not sure why EPWs need a special diet, I don't know why they can't just eat the same garbage we eat. I guess American MREs don't meet their standards, they need to eat better than us.

One more reason not to like these Iraqis. They get to eat better food than we do.

"You stink."

"Yes I know Leon."

"No, I mean really. You're really ripe."

"Leon I know!"

"What have you been doing?"

"I got up early and I went for a run, and the showers aren't set up yet."

"So. Hop in the water blivet."

"The water blivet?"

"Yeah. Hell yeah. 'Cause I'm not riding with you stinking like that."

"Isn't someone going to notice me sitting inside the blivet?"

"Yeah. What? So what. It's just the water they use for cleaning the equipment. It's not shower water or drinking water, so who cares. Just get in, no one is going to care even if they do see you. You need a shower just get in, go ahead, I'll wait for you."

"Alright. I'm going to do it." I leave Leon and I walk over to the water blivet. It's a huge inflatable rubber bladder that's filled with water. It kind of looks like a big grey swimming pool just sitting out in the middle of the desert.

There are hoses attached to the blivet that are used to spray off the equipment. A traveling car wash that is about to become my bathtub. This water isn't exactly clean, but it's not exactly dirty either. It's not clean enough to drink, but there's no cover over the water, so it easily fills with sand and whatever else is floating around in the desert.

This water isn't heated like it is for the showers, but then the last time I used the shower that water wasn't heated either. There's a heater on top of the shower that's supposed to heat it, but it doesn't always work.

This water is going to be pretty cold. It's early too, and it gets pretty cold at night and this water has been sitting out all night in the cold, getting even colder. The sun hasn't been up long enough to heat this water up yet.

Maybe I'll just skip it. So what if I stink. The theory that stinking keeps people away seems to be holding up. Leon won't even ride in the truck with me I stink so bad. Maybe I won't wash the stink off, I'll just smell today, stinking seems to have its advantages.

Screw it.

Let me just get inside this blivet. I can't get in here wearing my uniform and I'm not going to be able to climb in here naked, it's all out in the open at there's too many people around. Maybe I'll wear my PT uniform, it still stinks from this morning's run anyway. I can get clean and wash my uniform.

I run to my tent and change into my physical fitness uniform and head back to the blivet. I lean my rifle against the side of the blivet and hang my mask off the hand grips on my rifle and climb inside the water blivet.

I dip my feet in first to test the water temperature and my toes instantly freeze. This is going to suck, let me be quick about it.

I jump in with a splash.

I'm all in, I've got my head underwater and I'm freezing. I forgot to bring soap along with me, that's probably best anyway, a soapy water blivet might draw too much attention.

I use my hand and try to rub the dirt, sand and stench off as best I can. I dunk my head under water a few times and rub away the grime as fast as possible. My body starts to shake and turn slightly blue from the cold water. I give myself one more chilly dip under the water and I climb out.

Damn!

I didn't bring a towel with me.

I pick up my mask and rifle and make a dripping wet dash to my tent. When I get inside my tent I whip off my soaking wet PT uniform, towel off, hang up my uniform to dry, throw on some deodorant and change back into my BDU uniform. I head back to the vehicle and find Leon waiting for me.

"Ready?"

"I'm ready."

Leon leans over and sniffs me. "Yeah, ok, you're ready. Let's go."

I climb inside and take my place on the passenger's seat and Leon starts up the truck and we take off.

"So how was it?"

"Cold"

"Yeah well at least you smell better. Did anybody complain?"

"I don't think anybody saw me, so it wasn't a problem. If the water hadn't been so cold, it would have been alright."

"So, yeah, you can thank me anytime."

"Yeah ok, I'll get right on that."

"Come on now, my suggestion to clean up in the water blivet was the best suggestion you've heard all year."

"I would thank you, but you and I both know that my getting clean was for your benefit so you don't have to smell me. You ought to be thanking me."

"I should thank you because you don't stink?'

"Yeah that's right and you are welcome."

We arrive at the storage facility and we're greeted by the supply Sergeant. He's been running this storage facility for about eight months. He walks us through the entire facility and he's beaming with pride while he gives us the tour. This place, this facility is really important to him. He's really proud of the work he's done here.

But then I guess his world is a little different than mine. He hasn't left this facility in the entire eight months he's been here. All he knows about the war is how to supply people with what they need and he's been doing a great job of that. Would he feel differently about his job, about this war if his job involved killing people?

I guess killing people just isn't a part of his destiny.

Lucky bastard.

This is really a huge facility. There are rows of trailers lined up end to end. It's a big trailer maze in here, and everyone one of these trailers looks the same to me, I'd get lost for certain. But this supply Sergeant knows this maze by memory.

No map needed.

The Sergeant takes us to the trailer that's filled with the Iraqi food rations we came here to get. It doesn't take the three of us long to load up the back of our vehicle with rations for the Iraqis. My unit will be eating meals ready to eat tonight.

As we're about to leave the area, the supply Sergeant tells us to hold up for a minute. Leon and I look at each and shrug. I'm thinking, why not, what the hell. I've got nothing to do and nowhere to be.

Take your time Sergeant.

The supply Sergeant comes back with a carton of gum. Leon and I look at each other again. Gum? What are we going to do with gum?

This guy is really excited about this gum. He starts to open the carton telling us, "This isn't any ordinary gum. No, check it out!" He opens the package and big round purple and brown gum balls fall out and start rolling around in the sand.

"These are peanut butter and jelly gum balls."

Oh really?

He tells us to try them. Specialist Leon goes first, reaching for a purple jelly flavored gum ball and throws it in his mouth. The supply Sergeant tells him to put one of each in his mouth at the same time. "You want to get the peanut butter and jelly sandwich effect going on in your mouth."

Specialist Leon says, "I don't know Sarge, this one here kinda tastes like shit."

"Aw, come on!"

Leon grabs a brown peanut butter flavored gum ball and tosses it in his mouth. He makes a face like he's just stepped in shit and then he tells me to try it.

Yeah right. He's not making the PB&J combination look appealing.

"They're pretty good, once you chew on them for awhile."

This may ruin my ability to ever eat another peanut butter and jelly sandwich again, but I do it anyway. I take one of each and I toss them in my mouth.

These are the biggest gumballs I've ever seen. They're jawbreaker size, not gumball size. I start chewing, and honestly, the jelly isn't so bad. I bite into the peanut butter gumball and it blends in with the jelly flavor. I keep chewing and I cannot think of one single thing I've ever eaten in my entire life that has tasted this terrible.

I haven't swallowed the gum, but my stomach starts to resist and it starts churning getting ready to vomit in the event I actually swallow these gumballs.

I look at Leon and he smiles at me, he's still chewing. Does he really like the way these taste? He can't possibly like it.

The supply Sergeant livens up even more with the realization that we're still chewing the gumballs. He tells us he's got an entire trailer full of PB&J gumball crates. He tells us to follow him and he'll take us to the trailer. We can have as many as we want. We follow the supply sergeant through the trailer maze.

When the supply Sergeant heads inside the trailer, I ask Leon if he really likes the gumballs. Leon smiles and responds with, "Hell no, I spit that shit out a long time ago, I've been pretending to chew."

I tell him he's an asshole. The supply Sergeant steps back out of the trailer before I get the chance to spit my gum out. I look at Leon and he gives me a smirk and starts fake chewing again. What an asshole.

We load up our deuce with about dozen cases of gumballs, and as soon as the supply Sergeant leaves I spit out my gumballs and cover them up with sand.

We run into Lieutenant Sheffield and Leon offers him a gumball. Leon and I quickly glace at one another and we both start to pretend to be chewing on the gumballs. We convince Lt. Sheffield to try the PB&J combination. He agrees and puts them in his mouth and we try to keep him talking for as long as we can. As long as he's talking to us he won't be spitting out the gumballs.

Specialist Leon has a knack for talking endlessly about nothing at all. Leon's rambling on about who knows what and the lieutenant tries to make his escape, but Leon keeps pulling him back with his voice.

After Leon and I finish having our fun with Lt. Sheffield we head back to our truck so we can make the drive back to our unit.

Specialist Leon and I are driving back to our area when we get a flat tire. Usually if it's a rear tire that goes flat we can leave it until we get back to the area to change it. It's a lot safer that way and since all the rear tires are duals, we can drive with a flat tire or two for quite awhile without any real problems. But this flat tire is in the front, so we're going to have to change it now.

Leon and I stop so we can change it. There's just the two of us, so we can't really set up a perimeter and defend our location from the enemy while we're changing the tire. So we keep our M16 rifles and ammunition close by and get to work.

I take off most of my equipment and drop it in the sand. I lean my M16 up against the truck near the flat tire. Recalling my basic training Drill Sergeant's voice running through my head, reminding me to never let my rifle be more than an arm's reach away from me at any time.

While Leon is busy getting the spare tire out of the back. I take out the tire iron and I start loosen up the lug nuts.

I twist and turn the iron so I can loosen up the nuts and get them off. Some of them are on so tight, they don't move. I stand on the tire iron, putting all my weight into it. I switch back and forth from standing on it to pushing and pulling with my arms.

I get one lug nut that's tougher than an enemy fly, it's refusing to turn. I pull the tire iron towards me and the nut comes loose, and the tire iron slides out of my grip and slams right into my forehead with a loud smack and falls to the ground. No matter, I just keep working on loosening the other nuts. I didn't think it was that strenuous to the change the tire, but maybe it's hotter than I realized, because I'm sweating more than usual.

Spec. Leon comes around the side of the vehicle with the spare tire and he's got this weird look on his face while he's looking at me and asks, "What happened to you?"

"What? What do you mean? What happened?"

"Why are you bleeding?"

"Bleeding? Who's bleeding? Where?" I wipe away more sweat from my forehead and that's when I see my hand covered with blood. I hadn't been wiping away sweat that entire time, I'd been wiping away blood from the smack to the head from the tire iron.

I'm about to explain all this to Leon when I see him stiffen up and reach for his back. He lets out a painful moan and tells me he's been hit.

He gets another hit in the back of his left leg. I drop the iron and that's when I get hit in the left arm. It stings.

Leon yells, "Hurry up, get the shit out of the back!"

We both run to the back of the truck and pull out the crates of peanut butter and jelly gumballs. We rip open the boxes, grabbing handfuls and throwing them at our intended target.

We're getting hit pretty hard. We're being bombarded with the peanut butter and jelly gumballs and these little bastards hurt when they make contact.

Leon and I take cover behind the deuce and a half. Sergeant Valetta and the First Sergeant start circling us with their truck. They're making rounds around our vehicle, doing a drive-by gumming. We still got our flat tire so we're stuck here forced to defend ourselves from their gumball ambush.

I notice the 1st Sergeant getting out of the vehicle and heading for our location on foot. Sneaky bastard. Sgt. Valetta keeps circling us in the truck while the 1st Sergeant tries to sneak up on us from behind.

We have the advantage. He doesn't know he was spotted getting out of the truck. Leon climbs up in the back of the duce and he busies himself loading up balloons full of gumballs. They'll make excellent PB&J grenades.

With a forehead full of blood and a handful of gumballs I draw the 1st Sergeant towards me and into position so Leon can attack from the back. Our plan works perfectly. The 1st Sergeant is so focused on me he doesn't notice Leon is even missing and he doesn't notice him slip out of the back of the truck. We close in on the 1st Sergeant, me in the front and Leon in the back. Leon bombards him with fistfuls of peanut butter and jelly gumball grenades, while I continue tossing single PB&J bullets at him. I land one of my bullets right in the side of his head.

He has no escape. He tries to run, but he can't make it, he gets hit over and over again, he stumbles during his botched escape attempt and falls face first into the sand. Even with Sgt Valetta circling us and pecking gumballs at us, they're no match for our superior PB&J skills. We overpower our enemy and defeat them, sending them scurrying back to their truck to lick their wounds. The 1st Sergeant brushes the sand off his face and makes a retreat back to the deuce and they peel out as best they can considering they're driving a big two and a half ton truck in the sand.

Dirty bastards.

I toss a band-aid on my forehead and Leon and I go back to changing our flat tire. We hoist the flat tire into the back of the vehicle along with the jack and the bloody tire iron and we head back to our unit.

NINE

KISSES

I roam through the dark heading for my tent and I pass by the water blivet. It's the big collapsible rubber bladder that holds the water supply we use for cleaning our equipment. I hear water splashing around. What is that noise? Has someone else decided to use the blivet as their own personal bathtub the way I did?

I walk over to the blivet to get a closer look and that's when I see Sergeant Destino in the water.

"What are you doing?"

"What does it look like I'm doing? I'm swimming."

"Swimming?"

Sgt. Destino asks me if I want to jump in. I glance at Sgt. Destino who's wearing nothing but underwear and I think to myself, interesting. Sergeant Destino and me alone together in the water, wearing nothing but underwear. I could resist this temptation, but why should I? Why would I?

I take off my uniform, tossing it to the ground next to all of my equipment. The watchful, curious eyes of Sergeant Destino are on me the entire time as I get down to my underwear and climb in. It's really relaxing in here, the water isn't cold like it was when I was in here by myself in the morning. The water has had all day to bake in the sun and warm up and it feels good in here. It's like a hot tub. Maybe I should do this every night. Maybe I will do this every night from now on.

Sergeant Destino splashes water in my face and then swims over to me and grabs the back of my head and dunks me under the water.

I waste no time with my counter attack on Sgt. Destino. The water battle continues back and forth between us until we get closer to each other, a little too close and the mood quickly becomes serious.

The splashing stops and we move even closer together and find our arms circling around one another. We search each others eyes, our bodies wet and in the moment. Our lips come close together and our hands find each other's bodies, our hands roaming across each other's wet, slippery smooth skin. We wrap our bodies around one another sliding up close into each other, we are so close I can feel our what-nots touching, covered only by the thin material of our under garments.

It feels good, it feels real good and I take pleasure in the moment. A moment that takes me out of the desert. I haven't been this close to anyone in long time. It feels good. But I'm not sure if it feels right. What would a kiss lead to? Something more, something much more? Or nothing more? Isn't this exactly what all this tension between us has been leading up to?

Our lips move closer, ready to make contact. I can't help but wonder if here and now is the right place for this to happen. Maybe we should be somewhere else, maybe we should be away from this desert when we kiss for the first time. Maybe we'll never see each other again, maybe this is our only opportunity. Maybe I think too much.

I feel soft, smooth lips press against mine. A tongue eagerly parts my lips and I kiss back with a kiss that starts off gentle and soft and grows heavy and hard, along with other things. The passion between us increases in intensity as I'm pulled in closer to the wet body next to mine.

Our wet skin glows in the moonlight as our tongues swirl around each other's, exploring, tasting one another. I feel this kiss throughout my entire body. I feel lightheaded and a little tingly.

"Very nice."

"Definitely nice."

"Maybe we should get out before anything more happens."

"What more could happen?"

"Lots more."

"Maybe I want more."

"Maybe I want more, but this isn't the right time and place for more. If we're meant to be together, then we will be together. When the moment is right we will be together again."

"Besides if we stop now, you'll remember me forever."

"I would have remembered you forever anyway."

I climb out of the water with a huge smile on my face. I give Sergeant Destino a glace as I put my uniform back on and I notice the same smile across those juicy lips. I gather up all of my equipment and as I am walking to my tent I take a quick look back at Sergeant Destino who's still in the water. I rub my fingers across my lips, the passion between us tattooed permanently on our lips. I get tossed back into reality when I hear SSgt. Williams calling me over to the Scorpion Tent.

Damn. I sure hope I wasn't being watched while I was in the water. This could be embarrassing, we might even get into trouble, we're not even the same rank. I'm only a Private and Sgt. Destino is well, a Sergeant. Soldiers can lose their rank and be demoted for fraternizing with other soldiers like this. Not that I have any rank to loose, being a private and all. But still. Sgt. Destino has rank to lose.

I feel my heart speed up as I walk over to Staff Sergeant Williams' tent and prepare to get bitched at.

"Hey pumpkin pants why the hell are you all wet? Just what exactly have you been doing?"

Hell. Am I busted? Does SSgt. Williams already know the answers to the questions being asked? Is this a set up to see if

I'll tell the truth or try to lie? Shit I have no intention of telling on myself if no one knows what just happened. I try to think of a reasonable explanation for why I'm all wet. I could say I just took a shower, but my clothes are all wet too, since I didn't bother to dry off before putting my clothes back on.

"Soldier, quit messing around, dry off and get your crap ready to go, we've got a mission."

Well, shit. Are you serious? Why the hell did we have to mess around with all the sideways talk I could've been in my tent already. I walk away as fast as I can without busting into a run, the quicker I get away from SSgt. Williams the better off I'll be. No good can possibly come from spending too much time near the Scorpion Tent.

I'm almost to my tent when I hear growling. Growling? Can that be right? What is that noise? The noise changes shape into scratching sounds and more intense growling. I look around with the help of the moonlight and that's when I see the noise maker.

Is that a dog?

It's a black German Shepherd who's busy trying to get the cap off a water bottle that's rolling around in the sand. The dog has extra big paws that she hasn't quite grown into yet and her big chomping fangs can't quite get a handle on the bottle. The animal looks at me and then back at the water bottle and barks. I don't really speak the language of dogs but this one appears to be asking me for help with the water bottle.

I walk over and I pick up the water bottle. I unscrew the cap and tip the bottle so the water pours out. The dog licks and laps at the water until the bottle is empty.

Well that's that then. I start to leave and once again head to my tent and I notice I'm being followed. I stop and look down at the dog and she stops walking when I do, she sits down in the sand and looks away. Oh you're real sneaky. "Do you think I don't know you're following me?"

I start walking again and glance back to see the black dog with big white paws sneaking up on me. With an all black body and white paws it looks like she's wearing white boots. I stop quick and spin around to look at her and she stops walking and turns her head to the side, her tongue flopping out the side of her mouth. She's trying to act like nothing's up, I think if this dog could whistle she'd be doing it right now to reinforce that nothing's going on and I'm not being followed.

"Alright. Come on, let's go."

Her ears twist forward, she cocks her head and tosses her tongue back inside her mouth and she runs to catch up to me. We walk side by side to my tent, her white boots hitting the sand along side my black boots. I search through the dark tent and find my cot and sit down. I pick up the dog and sit her down next to me on top of my sleeping bag.

"You know for a dog that's not quite full grown yet, you're not exactly light." She responds by licking my face. Hhmmm . . . Alright, well a dog kiss wasn't exactly what I had in mind this evening, but I can't really complain about being kissed twice in one night even if one of those kisses comes from a dog.

"Are you hungry? All I've got is MREs."

I open the meal ready to eat that's been laying on my cot all day and I offer the dog the contents. She sniffs it then takes it into her mouth not even bothering to chew and spits it out onto my cot.

"Alright then. Sorry about that but it's all I've got."

She looks up at me with expectation.

"I haven't got anything else."

I look around my cot and glance around the tent. "Pringles? Do you like Pringles? Yeah of course of you do, everybody likes Pringles." I creep through the dark tent and I snatch the Pringles container that's sitting underneath Sergeant Evers' cot.

I sneak back to my cot and sit next to my hungry friend. I quietly pop the top on the can, the dog licks her chops, her ears perk up and she barks. "Sshhh . . . ." I raise my finger to my mouth and shake my head no. I look around the tent to make sure no one has woken up. I pull out a stack and lay them on the cot. She seems to swallow them without chewing then looks up at me and back at the can.

"Yeah they're pretty good aren't they? You want some more?" I dump half the can out on my cot. While she's busy making crumbs in my sleeping bag I start to get my equipment ready for the mission SSgt. Williams told me about.

Actually, now that I think about it, I wasn't really told all that much about the mission. I don't know where we're going, I don't know what we're doing and I don't know who else is going on this mission. I'm not even sure when we're leaving. That's actually nothing new, I usually don't get a whole lot of information about what's going on.

The only thing I do know is what to bring with me because that never changes, I'm going to bring the same things I always bring with me anytime I go anywhere. What will I bring? Everything. Like everyone else in the Army we always take everything we have with us everywhere we go, every time we go. We carry everything with us all the time, that never changes.

I dry off and put on a clean uniform, I hang up my wet uniform on one of the light cables so it can dry. Is that safe? Probably not. This new uniform isn't exactly clean, but it's desert clean anyway, which is pretty clean but not quite as clean as I'd like my uniform to be. At least desert clean clothes don't stink. Not that much anyway.

I make a quick check of all my equipment and weapons to make sure everything's working properly and nothing's missing. Then I begin the process of putting on all my equipment ensuring I have everything and that everything I have is in its proper place.

I look at my new friend, pat my uniform and slide my hands down the front smoothing out the wrinkles, "Well how do I look?"

She finishes eating the crumbs off my sleeping bag, belches and licks her chops.

"I look that good huh?"

There's nothing left to do now but wait. I could go find SSgt. Williams and ask what time we're leaving but that's really just an invitation to get chewed out. Screw it. They know where to find me when they need me.

Then again, if anyone comes inside this tent so late at night looking for me and wakes up everybody in here they're going to be pissed about it. I'd rather have just one person pissed at me for not knowing what time we're leaving instead of having an entire tent full of people pissed at me for waking them up. I'll go now.

What about this dog, what am I going to do with her while I'm gone? I wonder if she'll stay put and be here when I get back? She's not exactly a puppy, but she's not exactly grown either, I wonder if she plans to dig in the garbage and chew on people's boots, pee on their socks and do whatever else mischievous dogs are up for? I could take her with me. I look at her on my cot, curled up and asleep in my sleeping bag. I think she'll be fine right here.

I head out of the tent and look for SSgt. Williams and prepare to get bitched at. I should have asked what time we we're leaving when we were talking earlier, but my mind was occupied with more important thoughts.

My head fills with memories of that kiss. That kiss. What have we started? I could try to convince myself that we haven't started anything, that it was just a kiss and tomorrow both of us will have forgotten all about it and each other. But that's not true at all.

As soon as I get outside the tent I see a gathering of soldiers, I guess I'm right on time. I look at my watch. It's 1:37a.m. Great. Going on a mission sounds so much better than sleeping.

I head over to where everyone else has gathered. I glance around the group of soldiers that are going on this mission and I take note that every face I see tonight is male. What do these soldiers take note of when they glance around this group of soldiers? The first Sergeant is already in the middle of the briefing when I arrive, he's giving us details about what we are going to see once we cross over the border into Iraq now that the ground war has ended.

I guess the First Sergeant is trying his best to prepare us for the destruction and dead bodies we're going to see tonight once we cross the border into Iraq. But how can you prepare someone for that?

My unit's location wasn't far from the border during the air war and I heard the bombing. The bombs lit up the sky like fireworks on the 4th of July. The bombing was constant. The planes of the friendly forces flying over our position non-stop, back and forth, back and forth, making their trip across the border from Saudi Arabia to Iraq so they could dump their bombs and fly back to reload their ammunition.

Back and forth, back and forth, the sound of the planes flying over our position went on night and day. Bang. Crack. Lighting up the sky. Then the planes fly back overhead to get another round of ammo. Bang. Crack. Light up the sky. Back and forth, back and forth.

I don't want to say I got used to the bombing, but after awhile the noise didn't keep me awake anymore. After awhile the sound of the bombs hitting their intended target didn't make my blood shake. After awhile I started to tune out the noise all together. But I don't want to say I got used to it.

There has been a lot of destruction during the ground war and there has been a lot of Iraqi's surrendering. Too many, apparently, because there aren't enough Military Police to contain all the Iraqi enemy prisoners of war who have been captured or who have surrendered.

That's what we're doing tonight. We are going to assume the role of an MP. We're going to drive to a location where some of the surrendered and captured Iraqis are being held and then we are going to transport them to an enemy prisoner of war Military Police camp.

TEN

BUSSES

I'm not an MP.

I have no training to be a military police officer. I have no experience as an MP. I don't have the weapons they have. I have never worked in a prison camp or in a prison. I have never guarded a prisoner. Guarding and transporting enemy prisoners of war who have surrendered to the friendly forces is not going to be like engaging the enemy in a fire fight. I know how to fight, I know how to fire my weapon, I know how to throw a grenade and use my bayonet. I know how fight the enemy.

I don't know how to guard the enemy. I know how to kill the enemy.

Guarding someone means exactly that. Guard them. Keep them from escaping, keep them from injuring other prisoners, keep them from injuring themselves, keep them injuring other soldiers, keep them from injuring me. Keep them from killing themselves, keep them from killing others, keep them from being killed, keep them from killing me. Maybe I should move that last thought to the top of my list.

It's kind of like having a pet, you have to feed them, give them water, keep them out of the sun so they don't get too hot and dehydrated and become a heat casualty. You need to make sure they have adequate clothing and a place to sleep. You have to make certain they don't have any weapons on them and ensure that they aren't scheming, plotting or planning anything devious or deadly.

My mind is occupied with these complex thoughts of guarding prisoners as I walk to the vehicle and take the passenger's seat in the cab of the truck. I'd rather be driving tonight, it would give my mind something else to think about instead of being preoccupied with the Iraqi prisoners.

We drive through the dark desert in silence. My mind running through the long list of possible scenarios ahead of me. I'm not an MP, I don't have the weapons or the training they have and I'm not sure what I'm in for. What exactly am I in for?

It's late and I'm tired so this short drive feels much longer than it actually is. I try as hard as I can to keep my eyes open and I try not to nod off during the drive, but it's not an easy task. I'd rather be sleeping right now than riding around in the desert heading to a task that I'm not sure how to do. I wonder if the rest of my unit is having any of the same thoughts I'm having. They're not MPs either.

When we arrive at the location I see all the Iraqi enemy prisoners of war sitting in the sand. It's dark, but the area is lit up with several huge spot lights. There's a fence made out of jumbled up wire surrounding the prisoners. There are hundreds, no, actually more like thousands of prisoners here. Not a single female Iraqi, they're all males. I look at the MPs and I see that everyone of them are also males, none of them are female.

Maybe there are females mixed in with the crowd somewhere, but there's just so many people here right now I can't see them. I wonder why I am taking note of this and I wonder if anyone else here has noticed the same thing and if it matters? Does it mean anything?

It's cold out here and these Iraqi prisoners look cold. They're not properly dressed to be out in the desert at night, they're not properly dressed to be fighting soldiers. They're not properly dressed to do anything. They're wearing everyday clothes and they have sandals on their feet. They're not even nice sandals, they're just flip flops. These Iraqis look dirty, they look like they've gone even longer than I have without a shower and I haven't had a shower in a couple days.

The only talking going on here is by the MPs, how have they been maintaining control like that over thousands of enemy soldiers? Maybe it's all the weapons these MPs have, that'll do the trick. Having an M16 in my face would probably shut me up. I wonder what happened to all the weapons the Iraqis had? Where did they go? Did they leave them in their bunkers when they left and decided to surrender or did they hand them over to the American soldiers when they surrendered? Or do they still have their weapons hidden somewhere under their clothes?

These prisoners look like a tired bunch of soldiers. Are these people even soldiers? Did the Americans gather up a bunch of Iraqi citizens who were just going about their business, because they don't look like soldiers at all. I thought I had a hodgepodge missed matched uniform, but they don't even have uniforms. I wonder what they eat when they're buried deep inside their bunkers and foxholes. Do they have MREs, or do they eat something else?

Too many questions. I think I think too much. Let me just do my job and get this over with, because the sooner I finish this up, the sooner I can go to sleep. I hit the light on my watch and check the time. 2:43. I'm not going to be getting any sleep tonight. I unsnap my Kevlar helmet and run my dirty, sand covered hand across the top of my head.

The MPs start the process of putting the Iraqis on to the trucks. The Iraqis pile into the back of the deuce and a halfs. The trucks are already full, but the MPs keep shoving more on to the back of the trucks until there's standing room only. We have a limited number of trucks with us so they're going to have to make everybody fit on the trucks we do have even if it is cramped.

Now that I think about it, we got carted around on the back of deuces all the time in basic training and now that I think about it, we didn't even have this lovely canvas cover over the back of our basic training deuce. So, I think if it's good enough for me and my fellow American soldiers then it's definitely good enough for the enemy.

After all the prisoners all loaded up we're told to get ready to move to the new location. I climb back inside the front of the vehicle and my driver starts up the engine. There is a humvee with an M60 gunner perched on the roof following behind each of the Iraqi filled deuces. Each gunner has their M60 machine gun trained on the back of the vehicle and pointed at the Iraqis.

As I'm sitting in the deuce I realize there's not much of anything between the back of my head in the front of the truck and the area in the back where the Iraqis are sitting. There's just a thin piece of canvas separating us. Just suppose the Iraqis haven't been thoroughly searched for weapons, they could jab a knife right through the canvas and ram it straight into the back of the driver's head or into my head.

That one MP gunner behind us can't possibly see in the dark all the way thorough a pile of prisoners to see every small detail and sharp, pointy objects. Those MPs would have no idea what's going on while an Iraqi rips out a knife and kills us both.

Maybe they're content being a prisoner, they must be, why else would they have surrendered? They probably have no intention of trying to escape or kill any of us. Right? That's what I want to think anyway, but what do I know. Maybe this is a scheme so they can ambush us and kill us all. That's pretty risky though, if that is their plan, I don't think they thought that one though very clearly. Then again, they're desperate and desperate people don't usually think clearly. People who are desperate are just thinking about their most immediate need at that given moment.

Maybe killing us is their immediate need, maybe they received orders to kill us. I'd feel a whole lot more comfortable being behind the enemy instead of sitting in front of them with the back of my head sitting there like a target, separated by only a thin piece of canvas. My driver doesn't seem to care very much about the potential prospects of getting ambushed and stabbed in the back of the head. Maybe he just doesn't want to talk about it or think about it. But then he's driving so he has something to occupy his mind, I've got nothing, I'm just sitting here with an active imagination.

I slip my Kevlar helmet on my head and sit up in my seat, leaning forward as far as I can, getting my head and my back as far away from the canvas and the Iraqis as I possibly can. If I die, I want it to be a fair fight, I don't want die from a sucker stab to the back of the head. I guess it's possible for me to survive a head wound like that, how would that be though, I'd probably have brain damage if I survived.

I was tired before we started this mission, but I'm wide awake now. I'm too alert with nervous anxiety and an overactive imagination. There is nothing to look at in the desert. Sand and sand and more sand. If my adrenaline wasn't so amped up at the moment, the steady hum of this engine and the dark sky would be putting me to sleep right now.

I've got to get my mind on something else. Maybe not. Maybe my mind is just fine right where it is, that way I'll stay alert and be prepared for whatever comes my way tonight.

We make a stop so we can transfer the Iraqi prisoners from the back of the trucks on to busses. I guess this was the plan all along. The buses aren't able to be driven through all that sand that was back there where we came from, so we had to use the deuce and half trucks to pick up the Iraqis. Now that we're here where there's actual paved roads we can put the prisoners on the busses and transport them the rest of the way to the prison camp.

I don't see why they couldn't have just stayed right there where they were on the back of the trucks, truck, bus, who cares anyway? I don't. Like everything else that happens in the Army, I'm sure there's an explanation for it, an explanation that I'll never get. That's how it goes in the Army, I don't get all the information, just the whats, not the whys, I'm not important enough to get detailed information about why things are happening the way they are. I just get told what to do, how to do it and when to do it. I get told what to do a lot.

Now that we're here we need to do what we soldiers do best. We wait. The military police start unloading the prisoners from the back of the trucks and put them on the busses. They unload the trucks like they're unloading cargo or materials, not human beings.

It's a little strange, but I understand it. It's too hard to think of the prisoners as human beings because this isn't the way you're supposed to treat human beings and how can we do our job here if we start to think of these Iraqis as humans and start to develop compassion for them. I don't think we would be able to do our job.

So then, why bother to put them on the busses like they're human beings, we should have left them on the back of the deuces. Putting them on the air conditioned busses humanizes them.

The First Sergeant tells me to follow him. While we're walking he dives right into the instructions. It's late and I'm tired so I'm only half listening to what he's saying. We stop in front of the door to one of the busses and the First Sergeant says, "Any questions?"

"Wait. What?"

What just happened? Wait. How am I gona? I don't know how to . . . . I've never even. I see the back of the First Sergeant as he walks away out of my sight. With nothing but a trail of footprints left behind, I quickly scan my recent memory to see how much of what the First Sergeant just said to me that I actually heard.

I look away from the First Sergeant's footprints in the sand and I look up at the bus, I run my eyes across the windows and then to the door.

Alright well, ok. I can do this. I can guard prisoners. I'll just do whatever the other guards on the busses are doing. Right? Yeah. Yeah, of course, it'll be fine. I'll be fine. There should be at least one other MP on this bus right, and these MPs know how to guard prisoners. They know what they are doing, they've done this before. I'll just follow their lead. I'll do what they do.

I climb on to the bus. It's air conditioned. It's still early in the morning, so the air conditioning feels cold, but in a few short hours when this desert starts to heat up, that air conditioning is going to feel pretty good. But right now, it's just cold.

There are two or three Iraqis piled into each seat. How many does that make in total? Fifty, sixty maybe? I have a twenty round magazine in my rifle right now. I have four additional magazines two tucked inside each ammunition pouch. Each of them are filled with twenty rounds of M16 ammunition each. I'm not a very good shot with a rifle. I'm much better with a pistol, but I haven't got a pistol. I've got a rifle and rifles aren't really meant for close range combat.

If I fire all the rounds I have in my rifle right now and I have to reload and change my magazine, just exactly how long will it take for me to extract this magazine, open my ammo pouch, take out another magazine, load it into my M16 and begin firing again? The prisoners are too close to me. I won't have enough time to reload. So that's it then. Twenty rounds, twenty Iraqis and then they'll overpower me and I'll be the one with the bullet in my head.

The buss driver looks at me like he's been reading my thoughts. I give him a nod and a look that hopefully doesn't give away my current thought process. Shit if I get a bullet in my head this bus driver will be getting one too.

Well, I've got my bayonet. I could stab one or two of them before they kill me. Toss a grenade? Naw, that's a little over the top isn't it? I haven't got any anyway.

Wait. Wait a minute. There aren't any other guards on this bus. There are no MPs here. I can't be the only one, can I. Can I? I see the bus in front of me start to lurch forward and then my bus starts its slow crawl forward following behind the other busses.

Shit.

I look back at the Iraqis and hope they didn't pick up on my moment of uncertainty. I immediately get myself into a new frame of mind. One that will come across as someone who has done this task a million times before. I don't just tell myself I've guarded prisoners before, I make myself believe it. Because if I believe it, then these Iraqis will believe it. And right now, getting these Iraqis to believe that I'm a trained and experienced prison guard might just be essential to my survival.

I'm not tired. Sleeping is the last thing I could do right now. I'm wide awake. I stare at these prisoners and they stare back at me. I see their eyes and I look away, I don't want to look into their eyes. I don't want to see them as humans. They're soldiers, they're prisoners, they are the enemy.

I try not to let any emotion show on my face. I don't want to give anything away. I let myself go cold, emotionless. I'm here to kill them if I have to and they need to know that. I hope they can't see through to my soft, compassionate inside. I hope all they can see is a cold heartless exterior.

We drive on and the sun starts to come up. I'm blown away by the complex simplicity of what's transpiring on this bus. What does this bus look like from the outside? Just a bus full of people rolling through the desert. But on the inside, it's something much different. So complex on the inside. So simple on the outside. How many other things in life are like that? How many things or people look one way on the outside without ever knowing what's really going on inside?

The busses come to a stop, one by one. We're all lined up behind each other. An Iraqi prisoner of war bus convoy. How many times since the war started have the MPs rolled in here or to other EPW camps with busses loaded with Iraqis?

This MP camp is a prison for the enemy prisoners of war. A sand and wire prison in the middle of the desert. There is a wire fence all around the exterior of the prison. Razor sharp edged concertina wire runs along the bottom and across the top of the fence, surrounding the desert prison.

I cut up one of my uniforms once just trying to lay some concertina wire out, I don't remember even touching that wire and I was all cut up, the razor slit right through my clothes and sliced my skin. I didn't even feel it when it cut me. I did feel it when my drill sergeant bitched me out for ruining a good pair of BDUs. I can imagine what that wire could do to a body if you tried to climb over it or under it. My uniform was trashed, I had to throw it out, if shit like that can damage a uniform, it can destroy a body. All I did was get close to it, no where near anything like trying to climb over it or through it, and trying to do it quickly to make an escape, forget about it, it's not going to happen. Not without a shitload of slices and dices through your body anyway.

There are guard towers looking out across the sand filled yard. The prison is filled with Iraqis who have been captured or surrendered. They mingle around, standing, sitting in the sand, walking around between the wire fencing. The sight of these prisoners does something to my mind. This sight before me gets shoved away deep into my mind, in a place that holds certain types of memories. The kind of memories that you don't want to remember, but can't ever forget. That's the place in my mind where this memory is going even though I don't want it to, I can't stop it, I feel this becoming a memory while it's still happening. Maybe that's just how powerful this scene is, it's becoming a memory before it even finishes happening.

The prison seems to disappear into the desert. The wire walls extend for as far as my eyes permit. There are so many people here. Has the entire Iraqi Army surrendered? Why would people give up, just like that? Were they told to surrender? I wouldn't do it. No way would I ever surrender. Give up? Not in this life time. I wouldn't do it, I couldn't do it, not even if it was an order. But what kind of order is that anyway? What kind of a leader surrenders and then forces their people to surrender along with him? A shitty leader, that's who. The kind of leader who has no business being a leader.

Maybe they weren't told to surrender, maybe they just did it on their own. Maybe they didn't want to fight. Well, nobody really wants to fight. I don't want to fight, but I will, I do, I have been. Even though I joined the Army by choice it doesn't mean I knew at the moment I was signing those papers and taking that oath that I'd be here in the desert. How can anyone really know what their future has in store for them and how they'll act at any given moment? They don't. They really don't do they?

Every one of these soldiers here makes a choice to fight. Sergeant Russell that little bitch went crying home because he didn't have the balls to fight. Is that what it takes to fight, balls? Insanity? Instinct? Don't animals fight out of instinct? A perfectly calm, docile looking animal will rip your eyeballs out if you piss her off or get too close to her babies. Are women more violent fighters that men?

We make these choices everyday of our lives and we never know what we will decide to do until we actually do it. What makes one person make one decision and another person decide something different even when they're both in the same situation?

Sure men always get a rap for fighting and being violent, but if you asked yourself this question, who would you rather come across, a man who wanted to fight for the sake of fighting or a female who's protecting her babies?

Maybe that's why these Iraqis surrendered, they didn't have the drive that a mother who's protecting her babies has, because she will fight to the death. She will kill you unless you kill her. A man on the other hand who was just looking for a good fight isn't really fighting to the death the way a woman is, he's fighting for the hell of it. Does that make women better fighters, or does that just mean women are fighting for a more meaningful purpose?

If a man and a woman were both fighting and they each had the exact same meaningful purpose behind their reason to fight would they both fight equally?

Did these Iraqis just have nothing to fight for? No purpose, no meaning? Why are American soldiers so willing to fight? I have no personal stake in this particular war. I'm just doing my job.

I think I think too much.

It's starting to get hot now. I didn't see any showers at the prison camp and there sure weren't any shade trees hanging around in the prison yard. What would that be like to sit inside a prison camp out in the middle of the hot desert with no shade and no showers? I don't want to know.

I climb back inside the truck on the passenger's side. This has been a really long night. I wish I could say that when I get back to the unit, I'll be able to take a shower and go to sleep. But that's not the way the Army works. When I get back to the unit, I will be going to work. The Army doesn't care if you sleep and for the most part the Army doesn't care if you eat either. The Army definitely dos not care if you shower.

As soon as I sit down I become overwhelmed with fatigue. I become instantly tired. Maybe it was all that adrenaline I had and now that it's gone, I'm getting tired, like coming down from a caffeine buzz or what have you.

Now I'm glad I'm not driving, because I don't think I'm going to be awake for much longer. I don't think I could stay awake even if I had a drill sergeant yelling at me. I don't want to be rude to my driver and fall asleep while he has no choice and has to stay awake, but I just can't keep my eyes open any longer.

I hear banging. What the hell? Ahhh . . . Damit! I fell asleep. I snap my eyes open and look around my surroundings to see if I can identify where the noise is coming from. I tighten my grip on my M16. I must have trained my hand, because even in my sleep I'm able to keep a grip on my M16.

I realize I'm still sitting in the passenger's side of the truck. My driver looks at me like I have three heads. "What's your problem? Calm the shit down."

"What are we doing? What happened?"

My driver lets out a long tired sigh, "Detour. Let's go."

I climb out of the deuce and a half and follow behind my driver. It looks like we're in a city. I'm really disorientated, I'm still tired and still half asleep and the last thing I remember is dropping off some Iraqis at a desert prison camp and driving off into the morning sun with nothing to look at except sand and sand and more sand. So where the hell are we now? I didn't know this desert had buildings, but here we are in an actual city, surrounded by buildings and cars and people. People. Just everyday people going about their business like they have no clue there's a war going on. Where the hell are we?

I see a Kuwaiti flag at the top of a flag pole flapping around in the wind. We're in Kuwait? What are we doing here? I catch up to my driver. "What are we doing in Kuwait?"

I get nothing but the same lame answer I got before when we were still in the truck. "Detour" I even get the same exasperated sigh. That's great. Either he's a dick or he doesn't know any more than I do. I vote for dick.

I follow along with the rest of my unit who have gathered outside one of the buildings. As usual, we're getting a briefing. I finally start to actually wake up and I realize that there are only a few of us here. The rest of the unit that went on the mission last night isn't here. That's not a good sign, that could mean a lot of different things, but now that I'm fully awake I realize exactly what it means.

It means this little group of soldiers did exactly what my driver has been saying all along. They've taken a detour. And since I was asleep at the time the detour decision was made, I've been taken along for the ride. This is not a mission and we're not supposed to be here. But we are here and what the hell am I going to do about it?

I'm going to go along with it, because if I don't I'm going to be outnumbered and I don't know where the hell we are or how to get back to our unit from here. Even if I did know the way, what am I going to do? Leave? Take off in one of the vehicles? I don't think so, I can't exactly take off by myself. It will be better to just stay where I am and follow along with this group of soldiers who decided to take an unauthorized detour.

That'll teach me to fall asleep.

Maybe this won't be that bad. The group of soldiers begin to walk into one of the buildings. I reluctantly follow along. I take a quick glance around the outside of the building and down the street for anything suspicious. Nothing looks out of the ordinary and that seems strange to me. Everything thing on this city block looks perfectly normal. I really hope that's not a sign that something's not right. Maybe we're just so far from where the war has taken place that nobody here has been affected by it. I guess that's possible.

I just want to get this detour over with so I can get back to our unit. I know SSgt Williams is going to be waiting for us and I can picture the bitch session that's going to be coming our way when we get back to the unit. The longer it takes us to get back the worse it's going to be. I get bitched at enough around here the way it is now, I sure don't want to give anybody any reason to bitch at me anymore than they already do.

Damn. What about my dog? I left her on my cot last night before we left for that MP mission and she's been by herself ever since. I pull up my sleeve at look at my watch, 10:43.

Damn.

I hope my dog is still in the tent and hasn't caused any trouble. At least is she pees in the tent no one is going to notice. The whole tent floor is nothing but sand anyway, so that's good. One less thing to worry about. She's probably hungry by now though. I've got to get back and feed her. Maybe she's gone. Maybe she didn't think I was coming back and she ran off.

I'm going to have to give her a name. If she's still there when I get back I'm going to give her a name.

ELEVEN

PHOTOGRAPHS

I follow along behind the others as we walk towards the building that was once a firehouse. It's still a firehouse, it's just not being used for that purpose at the moment. It has recently been used by the Kuwaitis who had come here to escape, to hide from the Iraqis who were here to kill them, or to try to do things to them that are worse than death.

What's worse than death? If you don't already know, you don't want to know.

This firehouse looks like any other I've seen. A red brick building with two big brown wood garage doors set at the front of the building, a big flagpole sitting out in front. There's an entrance door hanging open off to the right of the garage doors.

I step inside the fire station and I quickly get separated from the others. I walk alone through the building and I head toward one of the rooms. I'm struck by the smell coming through the walls before I even enter the room but I keep moving forward anyway. The stench slaps me in the face the moment I walk through the door. It's the familiar smell of burnt flesh.

I look around the room and it looks like an old office, maybe this was the fire chief's. Grime is ground into the walls and the floor. I've seen garbage cans cleaner than this room. There's blood splattered across the walls and dark, dried pools of blood blanketing the floor.

There's a wire bed frame set up on chairs, the mattress has long since been discarded. The bed frame is attached to wires that look like jumper cables and a car battery. There's a lonely blood covered sandal lying underneath the bed frame.

It takes me awhile to recognize what this room is, what this room has become. This is no longer the fire chief's office, this is a torture room. I want my eyes to unsee this, but even if I could, there's no escaping the feeling of hatred that exists in this room.

I turn away from the hatred and I walk out the door, something the tormented Kuwaitis didn't have the privilege of doing, walking away.

I find the stairs and slowly make my way to the top. I still don't see any of the others that I came here with. Why the hell are we even here? What's the point in this detour anyway, someone's sick ideal of sightseeing. I just want to get out of here.

At the top of the stairs there are two long, narrow corridors, one off to the left and one to the right. There are several rooms hiding behind the closed doors that line the corridors. There's a thin railing opposite the doors that runs the distance of the corridors. I hear faint voices from below and I walk up to the edge of the railing and peer over the edge.

The open area below is in a shambles, expelled AK47 ammunition casings and garbage lines the floor. There's a ratty looking fire truck sitting in the center of the floor. There's pieces of plaster laying throughout the area, I look up at the ceiling and notice pieces of the ceiling are missing, no doubt those are the chunks of plaster that are now far below.

Several of the soldiers I arrived with are milling about the area, climbing all around and through the fire truck. I see my driver sitting on a big plaster chunk, smoking what should be a cigarette, but looks slightly off.

That's great.

I turn away from the mess down below and I keep walking. I see one of the doors set ajar and I nudge it open the rest of the way. Inside the room I see rows of beds toppled over and strewn about, clothes tossed around the room. Everything is in disarray, the remnants of a raid.

I try to piece it together in my mind. This is where the Kuwaitis came to hide, to save themselves, hoping the Iraqis would never make it this far into Kuwait City but I see the Iraqis did make it this far. I can picture it all in my head when I see the broken baby cribs and a dirty faced doll laying helpless on the floor, its little plastic arms outstretched in front of her like she's asking to be picked up.

I imagine the women and children tucked away here for safekeeping. The station overrun by Iraqis, the Kuwaitis taken prisoner, raped, tortured and eventually murdered. The children screaming, trying desperately to hang onto their crying mothers as they're ripped apart from one another. I exhale, realizing I'd been holding my breath. I shake my head, trying to clear it of the image, if only my brain were an Etch-a-Sketch, I could clear it of these horrible images with a simple little shake. I keep moving, what else can I do.

I leave this room and walk through the hall and that's where I see hundreds of photographs tossed all over the floor of the hall. There are pictures laying everywhere. I can't get through without stepping on them. I look at their faces, their happy eyes, smiling children and loyal pets, but no matter how hard I try, they mean nothing to me.

Usually when I look at pictures, even of people I don't know, I can imagine their lives. I can envision who they were, what they might have been thinking while the photo was taken, but not now, not with these photos. These people in the photographs are just empty faces looking at me, they're meaningless to me. This leaves me unsettled. Maybe I've seen enough, maybe this my mind's way of protecting itself, it refuses to let my heart see anymore, my heart has reached its limit.

I'm forced to see them as nobodies instead of innocent victims who were raped, tortured and murdered. I can't see them as people, people I got here too late to save. I can't think about them like that. I shake my Etch-a-Sketch head while I tell myself I've got to keep moving. I shuffle through the pictures, trying not to step on their smiling faces, but there's too many and my filthy boots scuff their birthday parties, weddings and family vacations.

One of the overturned pictures laying on the floor at the mercy of my boots catches my eye. It has one single word scratched across the back, Habibi. My love.

Have I got anyone I would call my love? I don't do I? If there were a photograph of me laying on a floor somewhere, would anyone care? Would someone look at it and see a happy face, would they see someone who is loved by somebody else? Could I ever be someone's Habibi? Maybe I need to be, maybe that's the secret to getting the Army out of you, having someone who loves you. There's more to life than being a soldier isn't there, especially when you have someone in your life you can call Habibi.

I walk into another room to get away from those photographs. More than anything though, I just want to get away from my thoughts. I wonder if anyone else thinks as much as I do.

I hear the voices of the others echoing though the corridor. I can't make out anything they're saying, just random words here and there. I hear a loud crash and then a moment of silence, followed by loud roars of laughter.

I keep walking and enter another room, this one is in perfect order, untouched, clean. It's a religious room. It's a drop of perfection surrounded by ugliness. I don't understand any of this.

What makes this room so special? The Iraqis don't disrupt this room, this sacred place where they honor their God. But one room over they torture and kill human beings and rip screaming babies from their crying mothers. This wall divides the rooms and separates good from bad. I don't get it.

I take my God with me everywhere I go. I don't have a special room to honor my God I take that with me everywhere, to every room, every place, everywhere I go, my God goes. There are no walls to distinguish where I can be good and where I can be bad.

I've got to get out of here.

The air in the room starts to feel too heavy to breathe in. I make my move toward the door and the faster I try to move the slower I feel I'm going. I walk through the corridor, shuffling through the photographs. I grip the railing as I pull myself down the stairs. I stumble on the last step, but catch myself before falling. My nose catches the burnt flesh as I move past the fire chief's office and make my way out the door.

I take a moment and breathe in the air. I need a cigarette, but I haven't got any. I walk over to our deuce and check the cab of the truck for any wayward cigarettes. I look on the floor, behind the seats, I look through the MRE bag laying on the seat, nothing.

I look at the dashboard and notice something I've never noticed before. A glove compartment. Do all the military vehicles have a glove compartment? I'm going to check on that when I get in another vehicle. I turn the latch and the door to the compartment falls open. Nice. Not only is there a pack of cigarettes, there's a book of matches, a small bottle of vodka, a fully loaded M16 magazine and a container of Pringles. What more could a soldier ask for?

I help myself to a handful of Pringles and unscrew the cap on the vodka bottle and tip it back. I'm good on ammunition, so I leave the magazine where it is. I take out a cigarette and pull a match across the back of the book. I inhale and let the smoke fill my lungs. I take another gulp of vodka and toss it back inside the glove box along with the Pringles, pack of cigarettes and the match book.

I climb down off the truck and walk up to the front of the firehouse. I survey my surroundings while I smoke. I check the time on my watch, 12:23. We're going to be in all kinds of shit with SSgt. Williams when we get back. I am not looking forward to that, at all.

I smoke my cigarette to the butt and flick the ashes and flame to the ground. I peel off the paper surrounding the filter and tear it into tiny pieces. I strip off pieces of the filter one section at a time, tearing from top to bottom like a piece of string cheese and let the loose pieces catch the wind any scurry off to a new destination.

The small entry door to the firehouse bangs open and the soldiers from my unit file out one at a time. This group is so loud, I hope they don't ever need to sneak up on anybody. So much for noise discipline.

My driver nods at me, "You ready to go?"

"I've been ready."

"Shit let's go then."

We all climb back into our vehicles, start them up and begin the drive back to our unit. I'm still not sure what the point of this detour was. I'm sure it served some purpose, whatever it was.

We leave the city and travel back through the sand to our desert set up and all the BS that's waiting there for us.

4:32.

SSgt. Williams is going to be beyond pissed off. I'm not sure what stage of anger comes after being pissed, but I'm sure I'm about to find out real soon.

I never thought I'd be happy to get back to my unit, but on this occasion, I am and I head straight for my tent. I feel a bit of nervousness in my stomach just before I walk through the door on my tent. I'm really hoping my dog has stayed put. I let out a deep breath and I walk into my tent.

I can see from across the tent to the other side where my cot is. There is no dog. She's gone. Shit. What happened? Was I gone too long? Did she run off, did someone take her or shoo her away. I take off my Kevlar helmet and hook it on to my water canteen that's hanging off the back of my belt. I let out another sigh and I sit on my cot.

I rest my elbows on my legs and let my head fall heavy into my hands.

"Shit where y'awl been? SSgt. Williams has been looking for you. I took your dog for a walk. I don't know I think she was kind of hungry so I fed her and gave her a glass of lemonade."

I raise my head from my hands and I see Leon standing in front of me, the German Shepherd by his side. I feel relief wash through my body. She's still here.

"Thanks. Thanks Leon."

She barks her agreement and jumps up on my cot like she owns it. She begins pushing my sleeping bag around with her paws, fluffing it up to perfection with her snout, walks around in a few circles lies down and closes her eyes.

"You give that dog a name? 'Cause I didn't know if she had a name and it would be a whole lot easier to call her by her name instead of just saying come here dog. You know 'cause that makes me look stupid and shit, you know what I'm saying?"

"Twenty-Three."

"What?"

"Twenty-Three. Her name is Twenty-Three."

"Twenty-Three? Yeah, ok, I like that. Twenty-Three. Alright, well, I gotta kick it, I'll catch you later."

"Hey Leon, thanks again, for looking after her."

"Yeah no problem. Catch ya later."

"Later."

I guess something useful did come out of that detour after all didn't it. I look at the ball of fur curled up on my cot. I got a name out of that detour. And that's not all I got out of it.

"Where the hell have you been soldier?" SSgt. Williams points at me with the full hand, not just a finger or two, but the whole deal, a full hand point. That's serious business. That's when you know you're in real trouble, it's like when you're young and you did something wrong and you get called by your full name, first, middle and last, you know you're in deep.

"Soldier. Soldier, I don't want to hear any excuses. Don't try to jingle jack me. I'm not falling for it! You think everyone else is going to do your work for you while you're out doing your shenanigans? Not going to happen. No. Not going to happen. You can do your own jack. Nobody here's going to do it for you."

How can this dog sleep through all this yelling? I look at Twenty-Three sleeping on my cot and I see a slight lift to her eyelids and then she quickly closes them again. You're not sleeping at all are you?

"Let's go soldier, you got work to do."

I let out a sigh and I follow along behind SSgt. Williams.

"What did you say soldier? Did you say something? What? No, ok good I didn't think so, let's go, let's go."

SSgt. Williams sniffs at the air. "What is that? Do I smell vodka?"

HELMETS

We're moving to a new location today. I've been awake since four this morning tearing down tents and packing up equipment. It usually takes a few hours to load everything on to the trucks and then another few hours to drive to our destination. Then it usually takes a few days to completely set everything back up again. It seems like when it gets hotter, it takes longer to move to a new location. Every thing and every body moves slower when it gets hotter.

I have help moving now so things are moving along a lot quicker for me than usual. Twenty-Three runs back and forth with me from the tent to the truck carrying tent stakes and light cords in her mouth.

We go back and forth until the heat gets to be too much. I have all my personal equipment piled up outside the tent, ruck sack, duffle bag, cot it's all ready to go, but it's the last thing I'll put on the back of the truck, that way it'll be the first thing I can take off the truck once we get to the location. All the stuff that got put on the vehicle first is way at the back by now, buried behind a bunch of equipment and tent poles.

I take a seat on my duffle bag and Twenty-Three takes up the rest of the space on the duffle, stretching her front legs across the bag. I take the metal cup off the bottom of my canteen and I fill it with water for her and then empty the rest of the canteen down my throat.

"Hey."

"Hey." I haven't seen Sgt. Destino since the night we kissed. It wasn't that long ago, but so much has happened since that night, it feels like it was a really long time ago.

"How you been?"

"Good. Busy. What about you?"

"Same. It's always busy though isn't it?"

Twenty-Three barks her agreement.

Sergeant Destino creeps closer to my duffle bag and I slide to the end of the bag making room for one more set of cheeks on the bag.

"What is that?"

"A dragon."

"You made this?"

"For you."

"Thank you."

The folded paper dragon stands guard between us on the duffle bag, keeping us from getting too close. Its long back twisting and turning itself into a jagged tail, its tongue flying out of its mouth like fire.

We sit in silence for a few minutes, soaking in the sun and the nice way it feels to have someone you care about close to you.

"Can I buy you a drink before we have to leave?"

"Alright."

Water is the drink we're both referring to and since we both have empty canteens we need to fill them before we leave. We walk together to the water buffalo, Twenty-Three and the dragon stay behind.

We pass by the First Sergeant on the way to the buffalo who tells us it's time to go, the convoy is leaving.

Sergeant Destino fills our canteens and we part ways.

"I'll see you at the new site."

"See you soon. Thanks for the drink. Next time I'm buying."

"Sounds good to me."

I'm a passenger again for this drive, that's fine with me, just as long as my driver doesn't decide to take any detours. The first Sergeant walks down the length of the convoy, pointing out the various flaws to all the soldiers as he walks past.

"Turn your headlights on."

Headlights in the daytime and no headlights at night. Yes, that makes perfect sense to me.

"Go fill your canteen before we go."

I already did that, so he can't yell at me for that one.

"Where's your fire extinguisher? Better get that where it belongs before we take off."

Mine's right where it's supposed to be.

"Helmet."

"Put your helmet on soldier."

Alright. You caught me. The First Sergeant never fails in finding at least one flaw with everybody. I can't stand this stupid helmet, it feels like I have a bowling ball sitting on my head. It feels so heavy I can barely keep my head held up straight sometimes. But we've got to wear it every stinking time we step outside our tent. I place the Kevlar on my head and secure it in place with the chin strap and snap it closed.

We drive on the mangled road, or at least what used to be a road. Now it's destroyed, the pavement's been torn up by bombs. There are trucks and automobiles pushed off to the side of the road, clearing a path down the middle of the road.

We drive our convoy down the center of the road, right through all the destruction. We're surrounded by it.

The desperation of the Iraqis trying to get out of the city is written all over the place. They were stopped in their tracks on their way out of the city. Their lives brought to an end in one particular moment in time, their very last moment in time.

Their vehicles bombed on the road while they were desperately trying to leave Kuwait City, but they didn't make it very far.

My feelings for them are mixed. They are the enemy. They are human beings. They had been running for their lives. The crews in the airplanes overhead who killed them are not here on the ground to see the destruction like I am.

I see them. I see the terror left on their dead faces as they tried to save their own lives, but didn't make it. I see their face frozen in time at the very moment they took their last breath. I see their vehicles still burning, I see their charred bodies. I smell their burning flesh.

But I also see their face, a human face, a face that belongs to a man who was doing what his country asked him to do, just like me. I'm doing a job my country asked me to do.

I try to hate this man, but I can't. I try not to think about him as a man at all. He is not like me. I convince myself he is the enemy, nothing more, nothing less. To think of him as anything else may drive me insane. To think of him as a man with a family will weaken my ability to do my job. I was sent here to do my part to defeat and kill the enemy and then I will go home and live a normal life.

I think maybe I'm already half insane to be thinking this way. But it's better than being all the way insane and having compassion for the people I've been sent here to kill.

It makes no sense to say it is a weakness to have compassion for human beings. It makes no sense that desiring so desperately not to kill anyone is considered a weakness. But this isn't a place that makes sense, and I'm not surrounded by friends.

We stop just past the burning vehicles on the side of the road. I don't even know what we're stopping for. This isn't our destination, we still have at least another hour of driving before we get to where we're going.

Twenty-Three is lying on the seat next to me, she's sound asleep. I feel this sense of responsibility growing. I feel like I need to take care of her. It's a new feeling for me. Caring about another living being. It makes me nervous. I know she's not a person, I know she's a dog. But a dog that is growing to depend on me. Maybe I'm starting to depend on her as well.

Twenty-Three starts kicking her back legs. She must be dreaming.

I look in the side mirror of the truck and I see Specialist Leon walking toward my truck. "What's up Leon?"

"Can you believe this jackass?"

"Who? What are you talking about?"

"Colonel Bahanda. This ass is sitting in the passenger's seat of his humvee eating his ham slice MRE and he tells his driver to pull over."

"Ok?"

"This clown wanted mustard on his ham slice and he couldn't find it so he tells his driver to pull over so he can find his mustard."

"What?"

"I'm telling you, this asshole stopped the entire convoy so he could put some mustard on his ham."

"That's messed up Leon."

"Smoke?"

"Alright."

I get out of my vehicle and I walked to the front on the truck and I join Leon who's already sitting on the hood. He hands me a cigarette and we both light up.

"Hey Leon, look at this."

"Who is that short little bastard?"

"Lieutenant Sheffield. He's pretty short ain't he?"

"He's a fat too."

"How much you think he weighs?"

"I don't know. 250, maybe. How does he fit that fat ass of his in those BDUs? I didn't know they even made uniforms that big. Didn't you fling shit in his face?"

"Leon, that was an a.c.c.i.d.e.n.t."

"An accident? That was funny though. Why exactly were you flinging around a shit filled shovel for anyway?"

"Well more importantly, why was he trying to sneak up on me while I was in the middle of a very serious mission?"

"Burning shit. That was your serious mission?"

"There is no denying how important that job is. What if no one ever burned the shit? It'd be all piled up."

"I wonder is he still pissed at you for that?"

"It was an accident Leon. Accident. How can someone be pissed about something that wasn't intentional?"

"Ha! They been calling him Lt. Shitface ever since. That's some funny shit. One thing's for sure, SSgt. Williams isn't going to be putting you on shit burning detail again."

"So. Something good came out of it then. Mission accomplished, no more shit detail for me."

"Is he walking over here?"

"Waddling over is more like it."

I start coughing out the smoke I just inhaled from my cigarette. "Here he comes Leon, I think he heard you."

"What do I care what Shitface hears."

"Specialist. Private."

Is that supposed to be his greeting? Well, alright then, two can play this game.

"Sir."

"Hey how you doing sir?"

Alright make that three can play this game, Leon's going to play too.

"Is it break time soldiers?"

"No sir, evidently it's ham sandwich time."

Leon really doesn't give a crap. Leon will say anything to anybody who's willing to listen.

Lt. Sheffield clears his throat, "Listen soldiers, I have a little task for the two of you."

"Two of who? I don't think so sir. That little task you got going on sir, I must delegate to the private over here."

"What the hell Leon?"

"R.H.I.P."

"So we're making up shit now Leon? What does R.H.I.P. mean?"

"Rank Has Its Privileges. The Lt delegates to the Specialist and the Specialist delegates to the Private. See how that works? So you enjoy your little task private."

"Asshole."

"Thank you and good bye."

I climb down off the hood of the truck and I toss my cigarette into the sand. I look at Leon sitting on the hood of the truck smoking his cigarette. He smiles at me and gives an overemphasized salute, ending with his middle finger in the air. Jackass.

The stupid task Lt. Sheffield wants me to do? Retrieve a helmet that's laying on the road next to a truck.

I hesitantly walk back down the road. It's just me alone on this walk. I could turn around and see the rest of my unit behind me and know I'm not alone. But I stopped looking behind me from the moment I left the plane. Looking back doesn't do any good, I don't bother with it anymore. It's a short walk to the truck, so I try to walk slower. This moment of mindless walking is very calming. A moment of peace that I want to last just a little bit longer, I want to stretch it out for as long as I can.

I let out a long sigh . . . Here I am at the truck. This single piece of equipment in the middle of the road. I hear Lt. Sheffield's nagging voice through the distance, wanting to know what's taking me so long. Seriously? Is he really going to start bitching at me while I'm in the middle of picking up a helmet for him? This guy can go fuck himself. What is this payback for the shit in the eye fiasco? Geez Sheffield it was an accident. Get over it already.

I check out the view, it's quite nice, all things considered. There's nothing but sun and sand for as far as I can see, with this crazy-ass road right in the middle of nowhere. How do these bastards not get lost? Well this bastard doesn't have to worry about that anymore.

I can hear the crackling of flames coming from the engine. The flames swirl up over the hood of the truck. I hope this shit doesn't explode. Who's gona take care of Twenty-Three if I die? Lt. Sheffield? He'd probably eat her.

The front doors have been blown wide open, they're hanging off their hinges. They're just dangling there, like a loose tooth waiting for that one last yank to pull it free. The inside of the cab of the truck is completely scorched.

Everything's scorched. I see the helmet laying on the ground next to the driver's door. The helmet is completely black. I pick it up and look it over. I notice I've left fingerprints on the helmet and the tips of my fingers are covered with ash.

I look down at the dead Iraqi lying on the ground, the flies circling around his head. I feel my heart falling out of my chest. The Iraqi lying on the ground was wearing this helmet when he went up in flames and took his last breath. I feel his death on my fingertips. I don't feel right touching the helmet he died in. This helmet, it's just like mine.

This stupid fucking helmet. The helmet everyone insists you have to wear in order to save your life. This helmet didn't do anything to save his life. This helmet is the only thing left of this man, and now it's going home with Lt. Sheffield as a souvenir.

I feel nauseous and I want to vomit but there hasn't been anything except water in my stomach for days.

I walk back to Lt. Sheffield with his souvenir. I'm already walking slow, but I slow down my pace even more. I want to chuck this helmet. I think about how I might not be able to wash this black ash from my hands no matter how hard I try. The black ash feels permanent on my fingers.

Lt. Sheffield is standing with a group of officers. I walk up to him and hand him the helmet. He smiles and walks away. I don't remember if he said thank you or not, I doubt it. I do know he either didn't notice or didn't care how sick the whole thing made me.

I walk away and head back towards the convoy and climb into the front of the truck and I find Twenty-Three where I left her, lying on the seat on the passenger's side. I pick her up and take my place on the passenger's seat and I set her in my lap. She wakes up briefly, but then quickly falls back to sleep.

I'm grateful to have Twenty-Three with me. At first I thought having her around was making me soft. Maybe that's true, maybe I am getting soft, but maybe she's just making all this shit easier to take.

Having Sgt. Destino around makes being here easier to deal with. It doesn't suck so bad when you have people or dogs around who make your day a little easier to take.

It's nice, it's real nice to have someone in your life to care about, someone who cares about you. But it also makes being apart from them difficult, I miss them both when we're away from each other. That's not something I'm used to, that feeling of missing and being missed and worrying about them, wondering if everything is ok.

I'm not sure if it's more difficult to have no one and not worry about them and miss them than it is to have someone in your life and then worry about them and miss them. They're both equally difficult for very different reasons.

I think I'd choose the having, the missing and the worrying over the other option. But then I'm not so sure you get to choose things like that. They just sort of appear in your life, they show up, just like that and then you do everything you can to keep them with you as long as you can. I guess you don't always get a say so about when they leave either.

It takes us another hour of driving to get to our destination and then the set up process begins. Of course, setting up is going to go smoother for me since I've got four extra paws helping out.

We put together as much of the site as we can before it gets dark. It's too hard to work in the dark without any lights and there's barely any moonlight tonight, so we won't be able to see a thing once the sun sets, which is going to be very soon.

Our sleeping tent and cots are set up, so at least there's that and we won't have to sleep on the ground tonight, that's always a good thing because there's too many insects around here to be lying down in the sand. There won't be anything left of your skin if you spend the night sleeping in the sand. Those bugs will gnaw away at every each of your skin. And with all the work we do combined with the heat, you'll be too tired to be woken up by bugs crawling across you body. You'll sleep right through it while bugs and scorpions crawl across your face, nibble on your flesh and suck your blood.

When you're tired enough you can sleep through just about anything.

FOURTEEN

QUESTIONS

I'm not sure what happened last night. I feel like I'm missing something. Everything's a mess. Twenty-Three's missing. I'm not sure where she went. Did she run away, did something happen to her?

I know I went to sleep last night. Didn't I walk inside my tent and lie down on my cot? I know I did. I had Twenty-Three with me, like I always do. I was in my sleeping bag and she was lying right next to me.

So then happened?

Why am I looking up at the stars in the dark sky? I'm still on my cot but where's my tent? Where is everybody? What's that noise? It sounds like popcorn popping. I don't know why my head is pounding like I'm hung over. I haven't had alcohol since I got here.

I can hear SSgt. Williams going on about respect for the helmet. Is this about what happened on the road with Lt. Sheffield? It doesn't make any sense to me. Why can't I get up? My legs feel like they weigh about hundred pounds each. Damn, my head hurts.

Let me just lie still on my cot for minute, while I try to make sense of all this. I stay put right where I am and I look up at the clouds and I wonder when it started snowing. Does it snow in the desert? Why is Specialist Leon standing over me, blocking my view of the bright sun?

I see Leon's mouth moving, but what I hear doesn't make any sense. Did I misunderstand?

"Someone took a shit in Sergeant Williams' helmet!"

"What? What are you talking about? Who's making popcorn?"

"What the hell are you doing lying in the sand? Where the hell's you're cot? How long have you been lying on the ground? Never mind, let's go, we've been ambushed, we've got to get the hell out of here!"

FIFTEEN

SOUVINERS

"Hey soldier, where you off to?"

I swing around to see Chief Morgan laid out on a hammock. It's strung up between two big deuce and half trucks and he's swinging in the middle with something that looks like a glass of iced tea in his hand.

"Hey Chief. I'm just headed back to my tent."

He takes a smooth sip of tea from his glass and lays his head back down. "Now why would you want to go a do a fool thing like that for?"

"Chief, you're laying in a hammock between two deuces and you know as well as I do that some clown is going start one or maybe both of these trucks up. Then they're going to drive off without even checking to make sure you're not tied up out here and drive off with you getting dragged behind through the sand and I'm the fool?"

"You see there, that's your problem right there. You don't listen. Now did I say you were a fool or did I say you were about to do a fool thing? I'd say there's a difference between the two, wouldn't you?"

"Alright Chief. Yeah you're right, I guess you did say it was a fool thing, you didn't actually call me a fool."

"I wouldn't waste my time calling anyone a fool."

"Why's that?"

"Well, I'll tell you."

"I thought you might."

"An actual fool is too much of a fool to bother to listen to anyone with any sense. That's I wouldn't waste my time bothering to tell a fool they're a fool when I know good and well a fool doesn't listen to words of wisdom. My words are too precious, I don't hand them out to just anyone you know."

"That I do know Chief."

"I especially don't give my words to people who are just going to throw them in the garbage anyway"

"I hear ya Chief."

"You know you have your own set of precious and profound words. So why do you keep them all to yourself, if no one ever hears your words, then they're not really profound are they?"

"You make an interesting point Chief, but whether or not anyone ever hears my words, it doesn't make them less meaningful. They still exist."

"What's the point, if no one ever hears them? Why have a talent if you're not ever going to use it?"

"What talent?"

"There you go again soldier, not listening."

"You mean my words? I have a talent with words?"

"You do. You're like me, you don't waste your words on people who aren't listening. You hand them out carefully, because you know how important your words really are."

"Well, I never thought about it like that before. I guess you've got a point."

"Yes. Of course I do."

"Well then, I'll just hand my words out to the people who actually want to hear them."

Chief Morgan takes another sip from his glass.

"What are you drinking?"

The Chief holds up his glass towards the sun and swirls it around, "What, this? Iced tea."

"Don't you need ice cubes to make that iced tea?"

"One would think."

"Chief?"

"What can I do you for?"

"Did you write a letter?"

"Well sure, I've written lots of letters, matter of fact I just wrote a letter to my wife day before yesterday. I sent it off with the lieutenant in the mail truck, but. Well, now I don't mean to name call or anything, but Lieutenant Sheffield doesn't give off much in the way of confidence in his abilities to deliver the mail. I do often wonder if the Missus receives all my letters.

"Actually, I was talking about a specific kind of letter. You know, I guess a lot of people here do that sort of thing. The letter you write to your loved one or loved ones and give it to someone else here to give to them in the event you don't quite, well you know. Make it back home?"

"Oh, I see, one of those letters.

"Yeah, did you write a letter like that?"

"I did, yes I surely did. Now let's see, I gave that letter to Staff Sergeant Williams, no doubt the Sergeant will make it out of here just fine. I chose someone that's too mean to get jammed up. Don't think too many people will mess with that sergeant."

"That was good thinking Chief."

"I know. Now, let's see, I've got two letters here myself. I guess two others around here saw fit to thinking that I'd be making it home just fine myself."

"I wondered about that, what if something were to happen to the letter carrier, how would it get to its destination then?"

"Well, I suppose in a case like that. Well, soldier, I believe I don't exactly know would happen in a situation like that. Let's hope we don't have to find out. Were you thinking about a letter in your possession or the letter you've written?"

"I didn't write a letter like that and when Leon tried to give me his letter to take home for him, I refused to take it."

"Why would you do that?"

"Well, I'll tell you."

"I thought you might."

I didn't do either because writing a letter like that or accepting a letter like that, is accepting the fact that you might not make it home, and that is something I just can not do."

"Soldier. I rather like the way you think."

"Really now? The Chief actually approves?"

"That I do."

"Was it to your wife?"

"What's that now?"

"Your letter, was it to your wife?"

"Now that is a question no one has to ask me. There is no one else on this planet I would write to."

"That's nice Chief. Having someone like that in your life. Someone that you love, someone that loves you."

"You haven't got anyone like that?"

"Well."

"Ah, your German Shepherd?"

"She's gone now. I don't know where she went. I don't know what happen that night and no one's seen her. I miss her Chief."

"Listen, soldier don't leave your heart in this desert."

"You don't have to worry about that Chief. That's one thing I will definitely be taking home with me, it's my souvenir."

"What more could you ask for to take home with you?"

"Twenty-Three. Sergeant Destino, maybe."

"Listen, if those things are intended to be in your future, then they will be in your future. Has it ever occurred to you that the lives of others don't necessarily center around you?"

"What are you trying to say? You think I'm arrogant?"

"I don't try to say anything. I say exactly what I mean and what I mean to say is this, you want Twenty-Three and Sergeant Destino in your life right?"

"Yes."

"Well maybe their lives have other paths to follow and you're not intended to be in their future. Perhaps their destiny isn't with you, they have their own lives you know. Would you want to keep them from fulfilling their purpose in life only to keep yourself content?"

"Content? No. Happy. Yes. They both make me happy."

"Let me fill your head with some thoughts. Your happiness is going to come by accepting what you've been given. It's not going to come from hanging on to what needs to move on."

"Everyone moves along their own path to their destiny, sometimes paths of destinies cross, that doesn't mean you should ever stop walking on that path. Even if you find something pleasant on that path. You have to keep moving because if you stop you're going to alter someone else's destiny."

"You mean because I'd be in their way if I just stood still on that path?"

"I think you understand me. Just move forward. Let's say you stay still on the path."

"Ok."

"While you're standing still, Twenty-Three and Sergeant Destino are moving forward and let's say it was intended for all your paths to cross again in the future. What will become of their destiny and your own if you stood still?

"I'd be somewhere way behind them.

"You wouldn't meet again in the future would you?"

"No. How could we? We wouldn't be able to, because none of us would be where we should be."

"Exactly."

"You're pretty deep Chief, you know that?"

"Soldier, I know a lot of things."

"Yeah Chief, how'd that happen, how did you get so smart?"

"I watch a lot of Oprah."

"Oprah?"

"Yes, Oprah. I getter smarter every time I listen to her."

"Hhmmm."

"If it's meant to be, then it will be."

"I came here with nothing and now I'm leaving here with nothing."

"Is that right?"

"You're going to tell me that's not true aren't you?"

"You're leaving with your life soldier."

"I'm not going to be a soldier when I leave here."

"Soldier, like I told you before you're a soldier for life. You can get out of the Army but Army has no intention of getting out of you."

"You really believe that?"

"Yes I do."

"Chief, do you think people can change?"

"No. No I surely don't believe they do. People never really change, it's your perception of them that changes."

"So, I guess you might think they changed, based on your perception of them even if they never do change?"

"Sometimes people just start making better choices than they did in the past and then you might tend to think they're different now. But they're not. It's perception that changes."

"Do you think there's any difference between how a person is perceived and who they really are?"

"Well, I tell you, the kind of relationships someone has between people and other living things, like say a pet for example, that determines what kind of a person they are. How someone deals with certain situations determines who you are. Be pretty hard to fake your relationships and stifle your emotions and reactions to things."

"So if you're really paying attention it's pretty easy to tell what kind of person you have standing in front of you?"

"You see, it's all about the connections you make with others throughout your life that matter most and it's how you cope with life in various situations that makes you who you are. This is what really matters in life."

"What about while we're here?"

"How do you mean?"

"Well, don't you think it's hard to be yourself while we're here?"

"Not at all. You see either you're capable of a certain behavior or you're not, changing your scenery isn't going to change who you are, and it won't make you start doing things that are out of your nature. People don't usually start doing things out of their character because they're in a different location. They keep doing what they've always done. People don't change."

"Alright Chief, I better get going. I see SSgt. Williams headed in this direction and if I get spotted sitting around shooting the breeze I'm going to find myself in the mist of some stupid detail."

"Well, alright now. I'm going to stay put, not much you can say to a warrant officer."

"Well, Chief, no there sure isn't much anyone can tell you is there?"

"I wouldn't listen anyway, warrant officers usually never do."

"Usually never. Nice talking with you, you have yourself a good day Chief."

"I believe I will. I believe I will."

"Soldier! Hey soldier I see you. I see you trying to run off. Don't think I don't see you."

Damn. How did SSgt. Williams spot me?

"I see you!"

Damn. Is this fool going to run after me? This fool is running! Let me pick up the pace, I got to get out of here. It's hard to run in the sand with my boots sinking in deep with each step and all my equipment jingle jangling around, bouncing and banging. I've got to find a place to hide, this Staff Sergeant is catching up to me.

I take a quick turn behind the Colonel Bahanda's tent and crouch down behind his humvee. Shit. That's the colonel's driver, what is he doing? He's coming right for the vehicle. Don't start it up. Don't start it up. Do not start this vehicle. The colonel's driver starts up the humvee and pulls away leaving me out in the open for SSgt. Williams.

"There you are soldier. You can't hide from me."

I get up from my crouch and take off running again.

"Get back here soldier, I got work for you. Get over here!"

Naw. No. Hell no. I'm getting out of here. I break off into a sprint, stretching out my legs and picking up the pace even more. The supply tent would be a good place to hide, but the showers are closer, I head for the showers. I make it to the wood box shower, lean up against the doors and catch my breath.

Still breathing heavy and sweating, I peek around the corner of the shower and scan the area for SSgt. Williams. Nothing yet. I might just be safe here. Let me just stay put for a minute until I know it's clear.

I'm standing still with my back up against the wood box when someone approaches me from the other side of the box.

"Hey, whatcha doing?

"Damn Leon! Where did you come from? What are you doing?"

"Nothing. What are you doing?"

"Hiding out. SSgt. Williams is trying to find me and give me some stupid detail to do."

"Oh for real? Alright then, I'll let the Sergeant know where you're at."

"You're an ass Leon."

"Why thank you."

Maybe he won't tell where I'm at. Maybe he'll just leave me be. It's possible isn't it?

SIXTEEN

BOTTLES

Specialist Leon and I are standing in the Scorpion Tent listening to Staff Sergeant Williams give us instructions on where to find an abandoned storage facility that's supposed to have several crates of drinkable water.

That's what Leon gets for giving away my position like that. Now we're both stuck on this detail, if Leon had let me be he wouldn't be going on this detail with me. I mean mug him when the sergeant looks away.

SSgt. Williams is still bitter about the whole shit in the helmet debacle. I don't know who would take a dump in a helmet, but since it wasn't my helmet that got crapped in, that's just funny.

It's hard to look at the sergeant and keep a straight face, because I keep thinking about the fact that there was shit in the helmet that's now sitting on the sergeant's head. I wonder did it get completely clean? It must still smell even it is clean.

The facility is only about a twenty minute drive away from our current location, but that doesn't mean it will only take us twenty minutes to get there. It'll take us a whole lot longer than twenty minutes to get there. First we have to PMCS our vehicle before we leave. If we perform the preventative maintenance checks and services on the vehicle the proper way, the by the book way, it will take us about thirty minutes to complete the whole process.

Leon and I have an accelerated version of PMCS and it takes us all of seven minutes to complete it. He checks the fluid levels in the engine under the hood, oil, transmission fluid, windshield wiper fluid, brake fluid and coolant.

I check the tire pressure and tread wear, I look underneath the vehicle for any major leaks. I only look for the major leaks because every military vehicle has leaks, it's nothing to get worked up about, it's like a little kid with a runny nose in the winter, they just always have one.

Together we check the lights, headlights, break lights, turn signals, blackout drive lights, those are the lights we use to drive at night. The blackout drive lights are supposed to give off enough light so that other friendly vehicles can identify that there's another vehicle in the vicinity. It's also supposed to be such a small amount of light that if the enemy is flying overhead they won't be able to see us.

Sure, alright. I don't believe it. But alright, whatever. Because if the friendly forces can see us, then the enemy can see us. It just makes it more difficult to be seen, but if you're looking for the enemy, which you will be if you happen to be in a combat zone, you'll see the vehicle.

I guess it prevents accidents from happening, because if you can see the blackout light of a vehicle in front of you then supposedly you won't run it to and cause an accident. The light sure doesn't light up the road any, so you can't see where you're going when you do drive at night, you just drive around in the dark. It's light out right now, so we won't be worrying about that at the moment.

Right now we need to worry about getting fuel because that's going to take us about an hour. The fueling location is about a half hour drive away and it's in the opposite direction from where we're going, so yeah.

Everything we do here takes such a long time, it takes a full day just to do something simple like fuel up and get some water. When I get back to the States, I'm going to go to the gas station in my pajamas, just because I can. It isn't going to take me the whole day just to put gas in my car and get a glass of water.

"Are you ready?"

"Yeah, I'm ready, let's kick it."

"You driving?"

"I don't care, yeah alright, I'll drive."

"Naw, I don't think so. I'm driving."

"Alright then, you drive."

"Oh, you'd like that wouldn't you?"

"I really don't care who drives. You want me to drive? I'll drive then."

"Oh no. No, no. I see what's going on here. I'm going to drive."

"What the shit Leon, are you going to drive or what?"

"Whoa, whoa, unwind buddy. Lighten up. I'm just messing with you."

I look at Leon and open my mouth starting to respond, realizing I don't have a response I just let out a long sigh instead.

"What? What's wrong with you? You'd think someone crapped in your helmet."

I ice grill him again, curling up my nose and my upper lip, I squint my eyes at look right at him.

"What is . . . What is that? That is your mean face? What are you mad for? I'm on this dumb ass detail with you."

"Serves you right."

"You're taking this a little too seriously aren't you?"

I shake my head, but I don't say anything.

"What?" Is this about your dog, you haven't found her yet?"

"No."

"Yeah, that sucks. No one's seen her?"

"No. And now we're nowhere near our last location. It won't do any good to look for her around here."

"She'll turn up."

"If she can, if she's not . . ."

"She's fine. It was probably just all the noise from the ambush that scared her off, the bombs, all the smoke, the fire fight. There was a lot of chaos that night."

"Yeah. Yeah, you're probably right."

"How's your head feel?"

"Aw, I'm good, it's just a scratch."

"You call that just a scratch? Alright then, it's just a scratch. Let's get the hell out of here and get this day over with so we can wake up bright and early in the morning and start this shit all over again tomorrow."

We pull away from our site kicking up a trail of dry desert sand behind us. I hope Leon's right. I hope Twenty-Three's alright.

I let my mind wander with thoughts. I'm glad I'm not driving. I wish I could remember what happened that night, I rub the side of my head, feeling the gash that was left behind for me that night, another souvenir I'll get to take home with me.

I know Twenty-Three's a dog, but I miss her and I've never had anyone to miss before. I've never had anyone around to lose before. I feel a deep pain in my heart that I've never felt before. I don't know what this feeling is. I guess it's hurt, sadness because someone I care about isn't with me. Sort of the same way I feel about Sergeant Destino, someone else in my life that I want to stick around.

We arrive at the deserted storage area. Besides the two of us there doesn't appear to be anybody else here. We walk through the facility, there's nothing here except the water crates. Some storage facility this is, it's not even a facility, it's nothing more than a location right out in the middle of the desert with a bunch of pallets filled with water bottles.

There are crates of water bottles stacked up about 5' high, wrapped up in plastic. The stacks of crates are gathered together in rows forming a maze. Most of the crates have been broken and the water bottles have been damaged. There are a few bottles here and there that are salvageable for drinking. We begin the task of sorting through the bottles, looking for ones that haven't been broken yet so we can bring them back to our area.

The wind starts to kick up and blow sand around the area and into my face and mouth. I take my goggles off my helmet and place them over my eyes. Then I pull out a green colored cravat and tie it around my neck and then pull it up over my mouth and nose to keep the sand out. On occasion I use my ear plugs to keep the sand out of my ears, but my helmet covers my ears well enough to keep most of the sand out.

I'm sorting through the bottles when I feel hot water splash across my back and soak into my BDU's. What the hell? I turn around to see Specialist Leon grinning, holding an empty water bottle.

Oh really. I unscrew the cap of the water bottle I have in my hand. Leon knows what's coming and he takes off. That's alright, I'll get him later. I'll get him when he's not expecting it.

I sneak around the corner of the crates and I climb up on top of the largest stack. I've got a really good view from up here. I can see pretty much the entire storage area.

I see Specialist Leon creeping around between the crates. I open up several water bottles and set them on top of the crate next to me. I line them up along the sides of the crate and I put another row right in front of me. I'm ready for Leon. All I have to do now is wait.

So I wait.

I'd like to think I've become an expert in the field of waiting.

Finally, my moment comes. Specialist Leon creeps through the crates, closer and closer to my position. He's right below me now, he never bothers to look up. I slowly stand up and line myself up behind the front row of bottles and I kick them off the crate. They tumble forward and land on Leon's head. Then I start grabbing the other water bottles and emptying them on Leon.

He starts tossing open bottles up at me, but I block them and they fall back down on top of Specialist Leon. He doesn't give up and keeps tossing them at me. I go to grab for another open water bottle and I get hit in the face with one of Leon's water bottle missiles. I lose my balance and I fly off the top of the crates, landing in a big puddle of water. The water's all mixed with sand, so it's really just a big puddle of muck.

Specialist Leon takes advantage of the opportunity of my moment of vulnerability and attacks at full strength. Dousing me with bottle after bottle.

That's when I see it. A scorpion, slowly creeping towards us. Leon must have seen it too, because I hear a loud "Shit!" And then Leon is gone.

I'm soaked, but this relentless sun will have me dry in no time at all. I think about the fact that we're able to waste drinking water by throwing it at each other instead of drinking it and the luxury of being able to waste drinking water like this reinforces that the war is over.

We load up our truck with all the water bottles we were able to find that hadn't been broken or emptied by one of us. It's a short drive back, and it's an uneventful drive. Uneventful is always good here. It's almost peaceful. I take off my Kevlar and lean out the window, letting my face soak up the sun. The single sound of the engine hums along with the peacefulness, kicking up sand behind itself as it rolls toward our destination. The engine is the only sound I hear, everything else is unusually quiet.

We arrive back at our area and Sergeant Williams is waiting for us. Well, yeah, of course I expected that. Without wasting any time we hear, "What in the hell took you assholes so long, that facility is only 5 minutes from here? I could've drove back to the States and took a drink of water from my garden hose quicker than it took you two dancing la-las to get water! Did you bottle the water yourself? Damn. Did you drive to a glacier and wait for it to melt?"

We open up the back end of the truck so SSgt. Williams can see how much water we got. "Well holy jingle bells, are you bastards telling me you were gone for almost 5 hours and this is all you came back with?"

Specialist Leon and I get busy unloading the back of the truck with the sweet sounds of Staff Sergeant Williams playing in the background, "Well holy train stations, can you caramel covered turds move any slower? This better not take you all damn day. You've got connexes to clean out when you're done with this. No, you know what? Yeah, take your time, stretch it out all dam day. You two turds can work all through the night. I don't give a jingle jack how long it takes you."

After we finish unloading all the water we get started clearing out the connexes. These connexes are just big metal storage boxes, the kind you'd find on the back of a semi trailer or on a train. It's hot inside, so we take off our BDU tops. I cut the sleeves off my t-shirt long ago, anything to keep cooler. As long as SSgt Williams doesn't show up, we won't be getting in any trouble for not wearing our BDU uniform top.

I'm mindlessly cleaning equipment out of the connex. Spec. Leon tells me to turn around. Hhmm . . . hmm . . . The last time I turned my back on Leon he doused me with water. But I do it anyway. He takes out a can of black spray paint and proceeds to paint the back of my t-shirt with a peace symbol. The paint soaks right through my t-shirt and onto my skin. Now I've got a black peace symbol spray painted on my t-shirt and on my back. It feels official to me now.

The war is over.

What's more official to the end of a war than a peace symbol?

Sgt. Valetta walks into the connex and tells us to load up all the crap on the back of his truck so he can drive us over to the fire. Sergeant Valetta started the fire earlier in the day and he's been burning stuff ever since.

We won't be able to take all this stuff back to the states with us, it's too expensive to transport stuff back to the United States, especially stuff nobody's ever going to use. All the important stuff will be going back, stuff like weapons, ammunition, tanks and vehicles. Well, the vehicles that are still in good condition anyway, some of them got tore up pretty bad by landmines. Those will probably stay here. I don't know how we're going to get rid of them, we can't exactly burn them the way we're going to burn all the rest of this stuff.

The fire is a short distance away from out unit, so it doesn't take us long to get there. We unload the truck and then we start tossing everything into the fire. Soap, toothbrushes, sun block, towels, socks, dirty, nasty, foul smelling socks. That's disgusting, who put their dirty socks in here?

Sgt. Valetta stands up, laughs and says, "Watch this shit." He tosses something into the fire and within a few seconds there's an explosion in the fire pit and a small burst of white foam. I ask him what he threw in there and he laughs again and shows me a bottle of shaving cream.

He has a whole case of shaving cream bottles. He throws them in one at a time. He hands me a couple of bottles. I turn them over in my hand and I think about the last time I followed along with Sgt Valetta's crazy-ass ideas, I ended up getting the Colonel's humvee stuck on top of a generator.

I pull my arm back to get as much momentum as I can and lob the shaving cream bottle forward like a football. I'm satisfied with my explosion and I toss another one in. Sgt Valetta throws the rest of the box with all the bottles in all at once. There's a large explosion and then a series of smaller ones. We watch the fire with satisfaction.

We empty out the truck and let the fire burn until it burns out. It's already dark, but it doesn't matter. The war is over so light and noise discipline isn't really important now like it was during the war. Supposedly the enemy isn't looking for us anymore. Supposedly there isn't an enemy anymore.

It's a strange concept. One day a certain group of people are our enemy because the president of the United States told us they are the enemy and then one day just like that the president tells us they are no longer our enemy. So what exactly are they now? Friends? Former enemies? If an Iraqi and I ran into to each other on some random street corner will we be friends? Are individuals soldiers able to put wars behind them as easily as governments do?

Too much thinking again.

I just want to turn my mind off for a moment and enjoy the randomness of tossing pressurized bottles into the flames of the fire.

We drive back to our area and I'm told SSgt. Williams needs to see me in the Scorpion Tent. Great. Now what? It's never good news when it comes from Sergeant Williams, and it's especially bad when you need to report to the Scorpion Tent. I feel like I'm back in high school and I'm being sent to the principal's office.

I reluctantly head over to the Scorpion Tent where SSgt. Williams is waiting for me. Who knows what the hell's in store for me this time.

"Well holy cat piss soldier, you're going home."

What? Really? Did I hear right? I'm not supposed to be leaving here for another 23 days. Can this be right? I don't really want to question Sergeant Williams, but . . . ?

"Got your orders right here. Pack your crap and get the hell out of my sight, you've got a plane to catch tomorrow and you're going to be on it. You've got roughly seven hours before your ride leaves for the air field, now get."

I get handed the paper work previously held in Staff Sergeant Williams' grip. I want to read it immediately, but I know better than to stand in one spot for too long when SSgt. Williams is around.

I walk back to my tent and I read the paper Sergeant Williams just gave me. I can't believe it, it is orders to go home. I've got less than one day left in this place and then I'm out of here, not even a day, less than seven hours. I'm not sure why I'm being released early, probably because this war ended much sooner than anyone had expected it to.

I walk back to my tent and I start to pack up all of my stuff. It takes me less than an hour to pack everything I own. I don't have much, and for the most part, I kept it all packed anyway. It's easier to move out quicker that way. But more importantly, it keeps the bugs out.

I lay my duffle bag in the sand and pile everything else on top of it, my ruck sack, rifle, Kevlar. A camouflage green holiday tree with a paper dragon highlighting the top of the tree.

Alright, well, I'm ready to go. I take another look around the tent and make sure I haven't left anything behind. Not that it really matters, none of this stuff is mine anyway, it's just on loan from the United States government I'm going to give it all back when I get back to the states anyway and anything I don't have they'll just charge me for it.

Now that everything is packed there is something much more important that I really need to do. I need to find Sergeant Destino. I received my notice to leave so quickly that no one knows I'm leaving yet. I can't leave without saying good bye.

I also don't want to leave without Twenty-Three, but I don't know what happened to her. I hope she's ok. Maybe Leon is right and all the noise scared her and she ran off. But then I've never known her to get scared. I don't really want to think about any negative alternatives, so I think I'd rather just believe she got scared from all the noise and ran off. Maybe I'll have better luck finding Sergeant. Destino.

I leave my tent and make the trek across the sand to Sgt. Destino's tent but I don't have any luck and no one seems to know where the Sergeant is.

Well, there are plenty of places around our site to look, so I do. The supply tent, mess tent, the water blivet, the water buffalo, the showers, the latrine. I'm running out of places to look. This isn't good and I don't have a very good feeling about it.

Not only am I running out of places to look, I'm running out of time. How is it going to look if I go tent to ask asking for the whereabouts of another soldier, especially now, it's getting late, it's after midnight. Will people get suspicious about what's been going on between us? Do people already know, or do people just think they know. Chief Morgan and Leon know, but I don't think anyone else knows. Would it even matter if anyone finds out now since I'm leaving anyway?

Since we're not the same rank we could really get into trouble for fraternizing with one another, but if one of the fraternizers isn't even here, what could happen anyway? Anything? Nothing? Everything?

I don't know. I don't mind taking a risk for myself and potentially getting myself into trouble, but I can't risk getting Sergeant Destino into trouble, that wouldn't be right, no matter how much I want to say good bye before I leave.

I pull up my BDU sleeve and check the time. I've got less than five hours before my ride to the air field leaves and I haven't found Twenty-Three or Sergeant Destino.

This sucks. I don't want to leave like this. There must be someplace I haven't looked yet. Maybe I should just write a letter and give it to someone and let them give it to Sgt. Destino. Who can I trust with a letter like that? Chief Morgan, that's who.

I go back to my tent and sit on my cot, I take out a pen and paper and I start writing a letter. I never thought I'd have someone to write to, but I do now. I take out my flashlight and I spend the next hour writing and rewriting, perfecting exactly what it is I want to say to Sergeant Destino.

What exactly do I want to say to Sergeant Destino?

I want to say a lot of things, and I want to stay in contact, but I don't have an address, I don't even know where I'm going when I leave here. I mean, I know I'm going to the United States, but where exactly in the United States I have no idea.

I guess that's something I need to figure out. I'm getting out of the Army when I leave here and I haven't given much thought to what I'm going to do when I get out. Where am I going to live, where am I going to work. I don't even have any civilian clothes. I've got a lot to figure out.

One thing at a time. Let me start with the letter and go from there.

What do I want to say? I put my pen to paper and start writing my thoughts.

It's late and I need to find Chief Morgan and give him this letter before I leave. He's gone too, where is everybody? There's only one thing left for me to do until it's time to go. I'm going to do what soldiers do best.

 SEVENTEEN

WAIT

I'm going to wait. Yes, I'm going to wait. Wait. I think I'm gona wait. Yeah, I'll wait. Wait. I'm going to . . . . wait. W-A-I-T-I-N-G waiting . . .

I'm waiting.

Wait.

WAIT.

WAit. wAIt.

WAIT.

WaiT.

WAit.

Wait. wAiT. wait.

Wait.

I wonder how many hours of my Army life I have spent waiting? I should really keep track of that, you know for my resume later on. I've got to put waiting on my resume. I'm an experienced waiter.

I stretch out on my cot to get myself in a comfortable waiting position and then I wait.

Wait.

EIGHTTEEN

HELLOS

I must have fallen asleep while I was waiting, because I find myself getting kicked awake by Staff Sergeant Williams, "Get up soldier. What do you want do, stay here for the rest of your life? The shows over, the credits are rolling, take your bag of popcorn and get the hell out of here."

Yeah, well ok hello to you too SSgt. Williams. I pull myself up to a seated position on my cot and try to avoid the glare of the flashlight SSgt. Williams is shinning in my face. I can't believe I fell asleep, I wanted to wait until it was early morning and then I could look for Sgt. Destino or Chief Morgan again.

"Have you seen Sgt. Destino?"

"Nope. Can't say that I have"

"What about Chief Williams, do you know where the Chief is?"

"Yep. Sure do."

I look up from my cot at SSgt. Williams hoping this isn't the end of the conversation and I am able to actually find out where the Chief is.

"Let's go soldier, you're short on time. Your ride's leaving."

"SSgt. Williams? The Chief? Where is he?"

"He's at the fuel point, left about forty minutes ago."

If I hadn't fallen asleep, I might have be able to meet up with Chief Morgan before he left for the fuel point and I could have given him this letter I wrote to Sergeant Destino.

I gather up my equipment, toss my duffle bag on my back and I sling my ruck sack across my front. All this equipment and these bags feel lighter than they did when I first got here.

I walk through the area one last time on my way to my ride, hoping to see Sgt. Destino before I go and hoping that Twenty-Three is ok and somewhere safe.

I really don't want to leave here without seeing Sergeant Destino. I don't want to leave things unsettled and that's the way things appear to be at the moment. Unsettled. It doesn't feel right to leave things between us the way they are. I didn't even get the chance to say good bye, to say I'm leaving, to exchange a phone number or an address.

Maybe things weren't meant to be between us, maybe this is it.

This is it. I'm leaving.

I didn't get to say good-bye to any of the friends I've made here, but I'm not any good with endings and good-byes anyway. No one except SSgt Williams even knows I'm leaving. Maybe it's better this way. People always say they'll keep in touch but they usually don't. I wonder if any of us would even want to. Do any of us really want to remember any of this? Well, maybe some of it. I don't know, I guess we'll see.

I load my stuff into the humvee and take the seat in the back. It's a short ride to the airfield from our location, but with all the sand and nothingness there is to look at it feels longer. Maybe it's because I'm leaving without what I really want to be leaving with. I didn't think there would be a moment in my life that I actually wanted to stay here in the desert, but I just don't want to leave like this.

What can I do? The driver stops the vehicle at the airfield and sends me on my way. I get out of the vehicle and don't turn around or even bother to say good bye to my driver. I'm leaving this place the same way I arrived.

Alone.

I pick up my bags and walk across the runway towards the plane. I feel the heat of the morning sun burn down on my shoulders for one last time. Bright sun and sand. I wonder if I'll ever step foot on a sunny, sandy beach in my life and I wonder if it will remind me of this place?

Worrying about whether or not I'll ever go to a beach, now that's a problem I don't mind having. I keep moving forward across the runway towards the plane.

I don't feel right about leaving without being able to talk to Sgt. Destino. I wonder about Twenty-Three, what happened to my dog, will I ever know, do I want to know?

Nothing about this feels right. I don't like leaving like this. I know I wanted to leave and get out of here, but not like this. I would stay longer if it meant being able to find Twenty-Three and talk to Sergeant Destino one more time. I would stay here indefinitely if it meant I could spend more time with both of them.

My feet hit the pavement of the runway, one boot in front of the other, I put all my focus on the task of walking, something that doesn't exactly need concentration. But I need to focus on something other than Sgt. Destino and Twenty-Three.

This is a commercial flight, just like the one I took to get here. It's all the same to me, a plane's a plane, but I think the food will be better on this flight than it would be on a military flight.

I reach the plane and look up at the stairs that lead to my freedom. I place my boot on the bottom of the stairs and I get ready to take that first step towards home and walk up and into the plane. With my boot on the bottom step, I hear it. Is it possible, or am I imaging things? Do I hear barking? I stop in my tracks and listen. Yes it is. That's definitely the sound of barking.

For the first time since I arrived here, I turn around. I squint through the bright sun, surveying the runway. That's when I see Twenty-Three, running full speed towards the airplane, her little legs moving so fast her body can barely keep up, her white boots hitting the pavement where my black boots just walked. I drop my rucksack and Twenty-Three jumps up in to my arms and starts licking my face with so much enthusiasm I'd think my face was covered with steak sauce.

I say hello to my long lost friend. She says hello right back to me in her own way. With tongue and tail. The dog way. I'm not sure who's happier, me or her. I sling my rucksack over my shoulder and carry Twenty-Three in my other arm. We climb the rest of the stairs and head towards the entrance of the plane.

The flight attendant greets us at the door with a friendly hello and gives us a smile, "Are you ladies ready to go?"

I look at Twenty-Three and she looks at me. Twenty-Three lets out an enthusiastic bark and I tell the flight attendant, "Yes, we're ready."

I take a window seat on the plane and Twenty-Three sits on my lap. I think about the old life I'm leaving behind and the possibilities of a new life in front of me. I think to myself, yes.

Yes, I am ready.

I'm ready to say hello to my new life. I'm deep in thought imaging what my new life will be like once I get home and I get out of the Army when I feel the seat next to me become occupied. I turn to look at my new neighbor for the plane ride home. My lips curl up in a huge smile of recognition.

Sgt. Destino leans forward to pet Twenty-Three and she wags her tail and jumps into his lap, he looks and me and greets me with a smile and says, "Hello."

"Hello. I didn't know you were leaving today."

"I didn't know I was leaving today either. It must be destiny."

34094548R00098

Made in the USA
Lexington, KY
22 July 2014